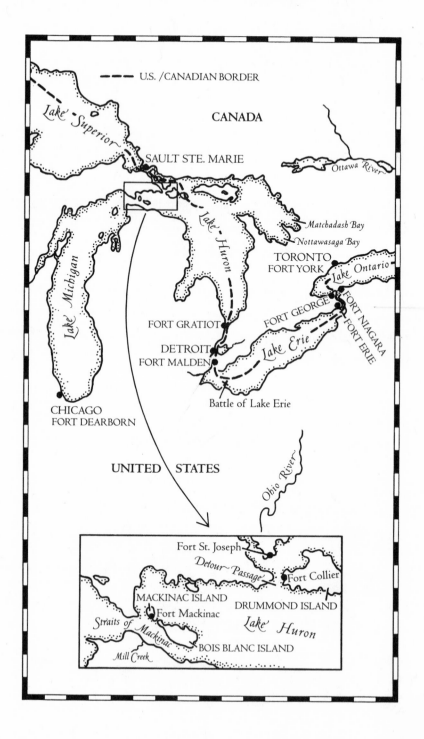

ONCE ON THIS ISLAND

GLORIA WHELAN

HarperCollins*Publishers*

Library of Congress Cataloging-in-Publication Data
Whelan, Gloria
    Once on this island / Gloria Whelan
        p.   cm.
    Summary: Twelve-year-old Mary and her older brother and sister tend the
family farm on Michigan's Mackinac Island while their father is away fighting
the British in the War of 1812.
    ISBN 0-06-026248-6. — ISBN 0-06-026249-4 (lib. bdg.)
    [1. Mackinac Island (Mich. : Island)—Fiction.   2. Islands—Fiction.
3. United States—History—War of 1812—Fiction.   4. Farm life—Michigan—
Mackinac Island (Mich. : Island)—Fiction.]
PZ7.W57180n   1995   93-13626
[Fic]—dc20   CIP
                                                            AC

Typography by Christine Kettner
Map by Patricia Tobin Fein
2   3   4   5   6   7   8   9   10
❖

For Barbara and Mike

CHAPTER

1

WE LIVE ON AN ISLAND and the world comes to us over the water. My brother, Jacques, was the first to look out across Lake Michigan and see the canoe carrying the traders. It was on a July afternoon and Jacques, my sister, Angelique, and I were in the field with Papa picking beans. The sun was hot, and our backs ached from bending over. We were happy when Papa said we might leave our work to go down to the bay and see the canoe come in.

It was the year of 1812. There was trouble across the ocean in England and France. A year before, a thousand Indians had camped along our shores bringing the pelts of mink, bear, lynx, buffalo, and beaver. Now fur trading had stopped and our island was nearly deserted. The canoe pulling into the bay was the first one we had seen in a week. It was only fifteen feet long, not like the huge *voyageurs'* canoes that stretched to thirty feet and needed a crew of fourteen. This birchbark canoe rode lightly in the water, so I could tell it held only a few animal skins.

Jacques could not wait for the canoe to reach shore but ran recklessly into the lake to meet it. It is how he comes to everything, with his whole heart. He is a tall, gangling boy and looked like a great sea bird thrashing about in the water. Although he is only fifteen, Jacques can talk of nothing but his wish to become a trader. With the help of his Indian friend, Gavin, he has built a canoe from birchbark and learned words in the Ottawa language. He shoots as well as Papa, but Papa says Jacques will do better to be a farmer like himself. "A trader must live on the land of others," Papa says. "A farmer lives on his own land."

The only time our island hears what is happening in the rest of the world is when some canoe or schooner arrives. On this day we were especially eager for news, for these were troubling times. Napoleon was marching across Europe. The English were boarding American sailing ships, taking American sailors away and forcing them to become members of the British navy. In Washington, President Madison was very angry with the British and was threatening war.

Even Papa left his work to come down to the bay. The blacksmith, Angus MacNeil, was already there and so was the surgeon, Dr. West, and his wife and their two girls, Emma and Elizabeth. We saw the Sinclairs, who have the farm next to ours, and Pere Mercier, the priest from St. Anne's church. There were even a few soldiers from the fort, which sits on a limestone bluff guarding the town.

My sister, Angelique, was the last to arrive. She had stopped to scrub the dirt from her nails and to bind up her curls with the green ribbon she keeps for special occasions. She is sixteen and thinks she is too old to have to work in our fields and soil her hands. I'm only twelve, but even though I'm a girl, I'm going to work our farm until the day I die, and get as dirty as I like.

The whole town gathered around while Jacques helped the trader, Pierre Gauthier, and his Menomonee wife, Marie, pull the canoe ashore. Accompanying the Gauthiers were two rough-looking men we had not seen before.

Pushing aside the townspeople in a most impolite way, the two men hurried toward the soldiers. They insisted on seeing Lieutenant Porter Hanks, who is the commander of the fort. They spoke excitedly, waving their arms and pointing off in the direction of St. Joseph Island. After a bit the soldiers led the men away to our own fort, Michilimackinac[1], at the top of the hill.

The rest of us gathered around Monsieur and Madame Gauthier. M. Gauthier is a tall man and as sturdy as one of the great pines that stand on the hills of our island. His black hair fell over his shoulders. In his sunburned face his eyes were as blue as bits of lake water.

Mme. Gauthier was as tall as her husband but slim and stately. She was wearing a calico dress whose bodice was trimmed with beads. Her brown arms were bare and covered with welts from the stings of the black flies. I have heard that the flies come down upon a campground to bite and bite until you run into the water to get rid of them.

1. Pronounced Mish-il-*mack*-in-aw

"What is the news?" Mr. MacNeil asked. He is always ready for a bit of gossip.

M. Gauthier was full of importance, waiting until everyone quieted so that his words should be attended to by all. "Everywhere we stopped we heard how Indians were making their way to the fort on St. Joseph Island to join the British troops. The Sauk, the Winnebagoes, the Ottawas, the Chippewas, and . . ." He looked at his wife. "Even the Menomonees," he added in a sad voice, for his wife is the daughter of a Menomonee chief. Traders often take Indian wives, for the traders live among the Indians, sometimes with the same tribe, for many months of the year. Their Indian wives can instruct them in the customs of their tribe and teach them the Indian language.

Mme. Gauthier did not look away. "If the Americans treated the Indians as well as the English, you would have as many friends among them as the English have." Everyone was quiet, for it was well known that when Americans traded with the Indians, the blankets they gave were thinner than those given by the British. And though it was against the law, whiskey often changed hands.

Papa asked the question that worried all of us. "Do they go prepared for war?"

As though the words were too frightening to say aloud, M. Gauthier nodded solemnly. We all looked toward the fort on the hill, it was our only protection. There, behind its limestone walls and blockhouses, Commander Hanks' officers and men numbered no more than sixty men. They could never hold out against a British army joined by hundreds of Indians.

Angelique hardly listened to M. Gauthier. She was looking up at a young soldier and fluttering her eyelashes in the way she practices in the mirror when she thinks no one can see her. The soldier was boasting to her that the British would never be able to storm our fort.

Papa shook his head at the boast. "No one will have to storm it," he said. "They have only to make their way to the hill that overlooks it." Papa had often warned the town that our soldiers did not command the highest point on the island but no one listened to him. Now he turned to me. "Mary, you had best go back to the farm and milk Belle. I want to go up to the fort."

I called to Angelique but she and Elizabeth West, who is her dearest friend, were giggling together over something the young soldier had said. Jacques was helping the Gauthiers unload their canoe. As I started up the path that leads to our farm I looked out at the two great lakes. Lakes Michigan and Huron flow together around the eight miles of shoreline that ring our island of Michilimackinac. You cannot tell where one lake lets off and the other lake begins. Together their arms are clasped around our island. Often what the lakes bring to our island is good, but not always. There is no knowing.

CHAPTER

*S*PREAD OUT BELOW me on the path was our village. Main Street winds along the bay. Behind it lies Market Street. Along the two streets the log houses nestle close to one another, in summer for company, in winter for protection. On Main Street is the church of St. Anne's and two taverns. In the summer evenings, when the doors to the taverns are open, you can hear the soldiers' shouts and laughter.

The largest buildings in town are the fur warehouse, the distillery where whiskey is made, and the government factory where the Indians trade. There they can buy calico shirts, blankets, axes, gunpowder, iron pots and kettles, knives, and the vermillion they use to paint their faces. Once our whole island was owned by the Indians but they sold it to the British for £5000.

Above the town is the fort. The island takes its time from the sound of reveille each morning at five and taps each evening at nine. Behind the fort and all around the island is a forest of tall trees. It took Papa many months to clear away enough of those trees so we could have a farm.

Papa and Mama came from Detroit to Michilimackinac in 1800, the year I was born. Papa said he wanted to start the new century on his own land. He came from Ireland to New York because the British, who ruled Ireland, wouldn't let the Irish people possess land of their own. Mama came from France. During the revolution in France, people had taken her family's land away. Papa said Mama and he were a perfect match. When the Americans chased the British from Detroit, Mama and Papa settled there.

My sister, Angelique, and brother, Jacques, grew up in Detroit. I was born right here in

Michilimackinac. I do not remember Mama because she died soon after I was born. Papa has a miniature of her so I know she was very beautiful. She had black curls, large brown eyes, and pale skin with little hollows in her cheeks. Angelique looks just like her. I have a round face and hair that Papa calls "ginger," but which is really just red. Because of the red hair I got cheated out of an elegant French name. I was called Mary after Papa's mother, who, unfortunate woman, had red hair, too.

Our house is just a cabin but inside the rooms are nicely whitewashed. There are blue-and-yellow calico curtains on the windows and hand-braided rugs on the floor. Our cabin has one large room with a great stone fireplace and one small room where Papa and Jacques have their bed. Up a ladder is the loft, where Angelique and I sleep.

I went at once to hunt down Belle in the pasture and lead her to the milking shed. Belle means *beauty* in French. I named her myself because of her handsome golden brown coat, the color of maple sugar. By the time I finished the milking and put the milk jug into a pail of cold water to keep cool, Papa and Angelique and Jacques had returned.

Angelique had baked bread that morning and with it we had a pork stew with onions and carrots from our garden. Angelique is a fine cook, fussing over everything. Papa dug a garden for her where she grows herbs. Mrs. West often sends her girls over to ask for some sprigs of parsley or thyme or even a recipe from my mama's book, which Angelique keeps in a pretty little box.

At the supper table, after first complimenting Angelique on the stew, Papa told us what had happened at the fort. "Lieutenant Hanks is sending Michael Dousman to St. Joseph Island to see what the British are up to. He is leaving at once."

"Won't the British be suspicious when they see his canoe?" Jacques asked. His mouth was full of bread.

"Jacques! Do not be such a *bête!*" Angelique scolded, using the French word for *beast*. She believes French makes a word more important.

Papa said, "Dousman is a fur trader and has business on St. Joseph. Hanks thinks he will not be suspected."

After dinner Jacques offered to take the eggs and milk down to the village store, where they would be exchanged for flour. Usually

Jacques has to be coaxed to do errands, but this evening he was anxious to go because he wanted to meet his friend Gavin and listen to what was being said in the town.

"Can I go too?" I asked Papa.

"Yes, but I want you both back before taps is sounded."

Angelique said, "I'm going to stay here and make an ointment for my hands. They are rough as a farmer's from picking beans."

"My girl, you *are* a farmer," Papa said. "Pretending to be something you are not will only make you unhappy." Angelique keeps reminding us that Mama came from the aristocracy, but Papa always says that is why her family had to run away from France.

Papa reached for a spill, a twist of paper, and let it catch fire from embers still hot from the cooking of our dinner. We all waited while he lit his pipe, for we knew from the frown on his forehead he wanted to say something of importance to us. "I have no wish to alarm you, children, but I believe hard times are coming. You have grown to be honest and useful. Should there be trouble I would not be afraid to leave the farm in your hands."

The sadness in his voice frightened me. "Papa! You aren't going away?"

"I did not mean to upset you, Mary. At the moment there is no need to worry about that. You may as well go down to the village and enjoy yourselves."

Although I followed Jacques down the path, I thought only of Papa's saying he might have to leave. We would be all alone on the island. I asked Jacques what would happen if the British came.

"I suppose they will line us up and shoot us, especially anyone with red hair."

I did not see how he could joke at such a time. "I am serious, Jacques. Will the British really take our island away from us?"

He looked down at me in a superior way that at another time I would not have tolerated. "They will try to get the island if they can. It's the center of the fur trade, and the fur trade means everything to British Canada. Besides, the British were the ones who built this fort. Michilimackinac belonged to them until America won it in the War for Independence. But just let the British try and take the fort back! I'll use Papa's musket against them." Jacques shook his long brown hair from his forehead in a way he has when he wants to show he is as strong as a grown man. Then he hurried down the path ahead of me so he would not be seen coming into the village with his little sister.

You could tell everyone in the village was restless for no one remained in their home. If you did not know how worried everyone was it would have appeared a cheerful scene with the blue water and the wide sandy shore and the people promenading back and forth along the main street, stopping to exchange gossip. In our town everyone talks to everyone else. Papa says if you live on an island you are like a litter of pigs nursing from the same sow.

Our neighbor, Mr. Sinclair, who even in the best of times wears a worried frown, was shaking his head at Angus MacNeil. Mr. MacNeil has the only forge on the island. So much time does Mr. MacNeil spend shoeing his horses, he brings with him wherever he goes the smell of the stable. He shoes all of the horses in the fort so he always knows what is happening there. He was saying to Mr. Sinclair, "The officers are worried about the British but their men pay little attention. If they have their card games and their daily gill of whiskey they are satisfied."

Mr. Sinclair said, "Some of the Indians who are friendly with the English left last night. I'm afraid they have gone to St. Joseph Island to join the British army."

While the men were talking, Jacques and Gavin and I slipped away. Gavin is really White Hawk. Or White Hawk is really Gavin. Gavin is fifteen, the same age as Jacques. He lives with the Sinclairs on their farm. Mr. Sinclair found Gavin ten years ago on the day before Christmas. Gavin's mother and father and some members of his clan had set out by canoe from St. Ignace on the mainland. Mr. Sinclair thinks the family was traveling to L'Arbre Croche, an Indian camp on the shore of Lake Michigan. A December blizzard stormed across the lake and everyone in the canoe except Gavin was drowned.

Mr. Sinclair had been fishing off our island and was making for shore in the storm when he saw five-year-old Gavin clinging to the canoe. He brought him home and warmed him. "A Christmas gift," he told Mrs. Sinclair. Gavin has been with the Sinclairs ever since.

The Indians on the island would have cared for Gavin, but the Sinclairs have no children and Mr. Sinclair is happy to have Gavin's help with his farm. Gavin told the Sinclairs his name was White Hawk. The Sinclairs said they couldn't bring themselves to call him that. They call him Gavin, for they are Scots and the name "Gavin" means white hawk in Scottish.

Gavin could tell little of his parents but tucked into his shirt was the dried head and wing of a hawk all wrapped round with string. After he was rescued, the Indians said it was a *pitchkosan,* a sacred bundle, which meant that someone in Gavin's family must have been of great importance in his tribe.

There were those on the island like Mrs. West who said the Sinclairs were foolish to take an Indian into their house. "Someday," she warned them, "you will wake up to find he has made off with all you possess. Besides, Indians are too stupid to learn."

That made Mr. Sinclair so angry he set about teaching Gavin to read. When Gavin had read all four of the Sinclairs' books, even the Bible, both Old and New Testaments, he was sent to Pere Mercier, who has a school for the older boys on the island.

Pere Mercier took an interest in Gavin and taught him Latin, which Jacques could never master. Sometimes, though, Gavin becomes

White Hawk and joins the other Indians at their camp. He is always hoping to find out who his real family was. Because his Indian parents called him White Hawk that is what the Indians and Jacques call him. You can tell at once that Gavin is an Indian, for he has hair as black as a raven's feather, and high cheekbones. He is slim and tall, but muscular, like a sapling that promises one day to be a great tree.

Once I heard Gavin tell Jacques that it made no difference that he put on the clothes of the white man, the white man still did not trust him. "I have not become that neighbor that Pere Mercier says you must love as yourself. I am no one's friend. When I go amongst the Indians, they say I am like the little tree frog who changes the color of his skin so that on the bark of a tree he is brown while on the leaf of a tree he is green."

Now Gavin had exciting news. "I found the eagles' nest."

"Where?" Jacques and I wanted to know. In the last month or so we had been watching a pair of eagles. Sometimes they soared over the trees, sometimes they swooped down to get the fish that were thrown away by the fishermen. Eagles are lazy and like you to do their work for them.

"At the top of a big pine tree. I'll show you."

Jacques and I followed him eagerly. The northeast bluff where Gavin led us was so steep we had to hang on from one tree to another to keep from slipping. There were briars that tore at my legs and arms, and once we scared up a fat raccoon that scrambled up a tree and hissed at us. The sky was darkening and just as Jacques and I were ready to turn back, worrying that we would be late getting home, Gavin signaled us to be quiet.

He pointed to a giant pine tree that reached up nearly as far as you could see. At the very top of the tree was a great jumble of sticks that was the nest. Sitting on the nest was an eagle. I could just make out its white head and yellow beak. I was thinking of what it would be like to live up there and see all over the island with one blink of your eyes when we heard taps sounded at the fort. That was our signal to hurry home. We slid down the bank, half running, and half falling. Gavin went to join Mr. Sinclair and Jacques and I raced up the path to our farm.

Papa hardly noticed our coming into the house late. I almost wish he had scolded us for he was just sitting by himself in the dark. All he said was, "You two go to bed. I'll stay up for a while and read." But he didn't light a candle.

I climbed to the loft, where Angelique and I share a bed. Angelique was in her nightdress with her curls up in rags and a pair of Papa's old gloves on her hands.

"Why are you wearing gloves to bed?"

"I made an ointment of hog's lard, rose water, honey, and an egg. It is said to make your skin as soft as a baby's."

"Where did you get the egg?" We weren't allowed to eat any of the eggs our hens laid. We sold them in the town or to the fort along with most of our vegetables and our hay. We needed the money to buy things we couldn't raise, like salt and sugar and calico.

Angelique said, "You must not tell Papa. I only took one egg."

"I won't tell if you promise not to take off those gloves and get hog lard all over our bed."

WHEN PAPA WOKE US I was dreaming
that the eagle and I were soaring together over
endless water. When I opened my eyes I
expected to see the sun shining in the tiny window of our loft. But there was only darkness.
"Quickly, girls," he called, "you must throw
something over your nightdresses and come at
once. Our lives may depend on it."

Angelique and I put our arms around one
another and held on tightly. Papa climbed the

ladder and stuck his head into the loft. "At once!" he said sharply and disappeared.

I slipped a dress over my night things and stuck my feet into my boots. My heart was pounding. "Hurry," I whispered to Angelique.

She was in tears, trying to unwind the rags from her curls but the gloves made her hands clumsy. She pulled them off. "I can't touch my curls! They'll get all greasy."

I yanked off the curlers while she complained that I was tugging too hard. Papa called to us again and we knew that there was no time left. Angelique followed me down the ladder, all the while fastening her dress.

As we hurried from the house, Papa said, "We are at war with England. Dousman came upon the British forces on board the warship *Caledonia*. They are headed this way. There are soldiers in *bateaux*, and canoe after canoe of Indians wearing warpaint."

Papa lit a lantern and began to hurry us down the path. We had started on our way when Papa saw that Angelique was not with us. "Where is that girl?"

"Here I am, Papa," she called. "I had to get Mama's box of recipes. The British shall not have them."

From every corner of the village we could see lanterns moving toward the western end of town. Babies were crying. Some people were talking nervously, others were silent with fear. We saw the Wests and their daughters, the Sinclairs with Gavin, and the MacNeils. Pere Mercier was trying to reassure people as he hurried them along. We learned the British had ordered Mr. Dousman to return to the island. He was not to alert the fort, but to go from house to house to urge everyone to stay in the distillery. The British promised to send an officer to keep us safe from the fighting.

We crowded into the distillery, startled by the odd things we were all wearing on top of our nightclothes. Men had pulled their breeches over their nightshirts and some of the women still had on nightcaps.

I had never been in the distillery before. The sharp, sour smell of the fermenting mash made me catch my breath. I looked around and found the Wests were next to us. I heard Dr. West say to Papa, "Matthew, our soldiers are outnumbered ten to one. How can they hold out?" He spoke softly so his girls, Emma and Elizabeth, would not hear the alarm in his voice.

Although Elizabeth is one year older and Emma one year younger than Angelique, their parents treat them like small children. They give them very little work to do and less to worry about.

"That is not the worst of it, Dr. West," Papa said, not caring who heard him. "The spring that provides water for the fort is outside of the stockade and unprotected. The British have only to take the undefended spring and in a few days the soldiers in the fort would be in peril from lack of drinking water."

"Papa," Jacques whispered. "Someone must warn the fort. Let me go."

He was about to start on his way when Papa reached out and seized his arm. "Do not be foolish, Jacques," Papa said in a stern voice, and then more softly, "someone is already on the way to the fort." With a sigh he added, "Much good it will do."

Mr. MacNeil said, "The British know that if they can take Michilimackinac they will control Canada and the fur trade. They have an experienced officer in Captain Roberts. He has fought in India and Ceylon. He will know how to do the job."

The words *India* and *Ceylon* were magic to me. I forgot for a moment that Captain Roberts was our enemy. I longed to see this man who had been in such faraway places.

Mr. Sinclair, our neighbor who has no love for the British, said in an angry voice, "I cannot think why runners were not sent from Detroit to let us know that America and Britain were at war."

Suddenly, standing before us was a British officer in his red coat and white breeches, a sword at his side and a musket slung over his shoulder. For a moment there was silence. Mr. Sinclair looked as though he might set upon the British officer and thrash him. It was Pere Mercier who addressed the officer. "Sir, are you the guard who has been sent to see that we are safe?"

"I am, Father," the officer said. "Our men have landed on the northwest side of the island and even now are marching through the woods to the high ground that overlooks the fort. They have two six-pound cannons with them."

Papa caught his breath. "If you open fire on the fort with those cannons you will kill every-one in it." I thought of how many times Papa had said that the fort was never safe as long as there was undefended higher ground.

"I hope, sir, that it will not come to that."

And the soldier really did sound as if he hoped it would not. Just then we heard the boom of a gun and we all cried out

"Just a warning," the officer said. "Do not trouble yourselves."

We held our breath but no cannon answered the blast and no further boom was heard.

"Can it be," Mr. MacNeil asked, "that Lieutenant Hanks has surrendered the fort so quickly? If the British take over Michilimackinac we will surely be required to become British citizens."

"Never!" Papa said. He looked so ready to run to the fort's defense that the British officer lifted his musket in warning.

"What other choice is there?" Dr. West asked. He certainly sounded as if he himself had given up.

When nothing further was heard from the fort we began to move outside, anxious for a breath of fresh air. It had been dark when we had gathered. Now the morning sun was shining brightly as though it had no idea that our world was coming to an end. We all stood silently look-ing up at the fort.

Hardly daring to breathe we watched as the gate of the fort opened. Three men marched out carrying the white flag of truce. Soon after the American flag was lowered on the staff above the fort. Every day of my life I had looked up to see the Stars and Stripes fluttering in the breeze. I believed it would be there forever. Now forever had ended.

CHAPTER

E WERE ALL DRAWN to the fort, anxious to hear what was to become of us. At noon
Lieutenant Hanks and his officers and men,
dressed in their best blue uniforms, marched out
of the fort with the Honors of War. The British
soldiers in their red jackets marched into the
fort. Soon the Union Jack was flying from the
staff.

As the British flag was raised we heard muskets firing down on the bay. At first we feared

fighting had broken out but it was only the Canadians and Indians come to join the British forces. Their canoes were rounding the island, each canoe flying tatters of cloth in the British colors. Hundreds of Indians ran upon the shore cheering and shouting in a most frightening way. Their faces and bodies were painted with vermilion and their long hair was caught back and stuck with feathers. Seeing hundreds of warriors leaping out of their canoes we were afraid, but the Indians only wished to shout and dance. They romped and frolicked about, setting off their muskets into the air. In the fort the British soldiers fired off the cannons to answer this merrymaking.

Papa looked grim. "The British will take pleasure in capturing those cannons," he said. "Those are the very cannons that were taken from the British thirty years ago at the battle of Yorktown when America was fighting England for its independence."

Gavin was the only Indian amongst us. As we watched the Indian warriors on the beach there were those who looked unkindly on him even though he was on our side. I think he saw this for after a bit he turned to go back to the Sinclairs' farm. Jacques followed him.

There was so much noise on the island I couldn't think. It just about broke my heart to watch the other side celebrate. Worst of all some of our friends like the Wests and the MacNeils seemed almost to welcome the British. Mr. MacNeil said that he had heard they had fine horses which would be a pleasure to shoe.

Mrs. West and her girls had gone home and returned in their good clothes, as if we were having a party instead of losing a war. "I am sure," Mrs. West said, "that things at the fort will be a little more civilized now. The British officers are so well bred."

Papa could not stop himself from saying, "Madam, if you are saying our American soldiers are vulgar, you are not only unkind to them, you dishonor them."

Dr. West was upon Papa at once. "Sir, do you accuse my wife of untruthfulness?"

Papa's face was stormy with anger. "The American soldier who soundly defeated the British soldier in our War for Independence does not need me to defend him." Then he grabbed me by the arm, and shepherding Angelique also, marched us back to the farm.

That evening a British soldier knocked at our door. I held my breath, afraid someone had told how Papa had stood up for our side. Perhaps the soldier had come to take Papa away. Instead he was there because he had heard we had a cow and some pigs. He wanted to buy them. The soldier, who was very young, explained, "Captain Roberts is having a big celebration for his men at the fort."

The soldier looked around at our farm and pronounced it a fine one. "Back in England I was raised on a farm and I know a good one when I see it." He could not keep his eyes from Angelique and every time he looked at her he blushed.

Although the soldier was more than polite, Papa growled at him. "Sir, my farm stock is not for sale to the British."

We were afraid Papa's words would make the soldier angry but he just bowed. With one more look at Angelique he said, "No harm done, sir," and left us.

"He seemed a friendly man," Angelique said.

Papa is always tender toward Angelique. I believe that is because she looks so much like my mama. Now he startled us by speaking to her in an angry voice. "You are as bad as Mrs. West. You will change your loyalty for a pleasant look."

Angelique began to cry. I did, too, for Papa had never been so cross at one of us. Jacques, who can't bear a quarrel, hurried outside.

At once Papa was sorry. "There may be things for which I will forgive the British but I will never forgive them for making me lose my temper with my own children." He looked so unhappy that Angelique and I could only cry all the harder.

CHAPTER

5

*I*N THE DAYS that followed there was much unhappiness. Captain Roberts sent out an order from the fort that all the adult men on the island must take an Oath of Allegiance to the British or leave Michilimackinac. Neighbor turned against neighbor. Dr. West took the oath. "How can I leave the island and the fort," he asked, "with no one to care for the sick?" Mr. MacNeil was offered the job of blacksmith for the fort and he took the oath.

The Sinclairs were leaving. They begged Gavin to go with them but he would not. "I must stay here. I cannot leave this island until I learn who my people are."

"But surely we are your people now," Mrs. Sinclair pleaded. She is a timid woman with velvet eyes and soft ways. I did not see how Gavin could refuse her.

But Gavin would not change his mind. "I will stay here and watch over your farm." And the Sinclairs had to be satisfied with that.

Pere Mercier was staying. "The church has no country," he said. The government agent also refused to take the oath. He had said that all the furs and the Indian trading goods in the factory were United States property. Captain Roberts said it was public property. He took it all and gave it to the Indians as reward for fighting on the British side.

Defeat was hard on the American soldiers. Some of them had been British subjects before becoming Americans. The British would not recognize their American citizenship and forced the soldiers, against their will, into the British army. Three of those soldiers were accused of being deserters from the British army. We feared that they would be shot. Luckily they were clever with the drum and fife. Since the British had no drummer or fifer the men were put to work at their trade and their lives spared.

Jacques, Angelique, and I could only think about what Papa might do. "I would not mind going to Detroit. French is much spoken there," said Angelique. "I was very young when we lived in Detroit but I remember seeing one of the great men of the town. He powdered his hair and wore an embroidered waistcoat of silk, and breeches with silver buckles at the knee."

Jacques groaned. "I'd rather be shot than live near such a fop. If Papa says we must go back to Detroit I'll head for the west where you needn't comb your hair or change your clothes from one month to the next."

"They'll have to drag me off of the island," I said. "Papa told me that in Detroit Mama's gown was soiled by a man who sat next to her in church and spat tobacco juice. I'll never leave this farm to go to a city where people spit tobacco juice all over you."

Although I waited from minute to minute to hear what he would say, it was not until the end of the week that Papa finally told us what he meant to do. Because it was Friday our meal was a lean one, for the church said on that day we must have no meat with our meals. Angelique had made a soup of whitefish with onions and potatoes. There was cornbread and wild raspberries that Gavin and I had picked that afternoon.

After our dinner was over, Angelique began to gather up our bowls. Papa stopped her. "Sit down, child, I must have a serious talk with the three of you." Angelique quickly slid into her chair. Jacques looked at the door as though he were ready to bolt right through it. Jacques hates serious talks. I held my breath.

Papa had a stern look on his face. "I will not take an oath of allegiance to the British. I am an American and I will stay an American. I am going to Detroit. If they will have me, I will join our country's army."

"Papa," Angelique cried, "you will be killed by the British!"

"I'm going with you, Papa!" Jacques declared. "I'm old enough to fight."

I was too frightened to say a word. I could not believe that Papa would go away and leave us. Finally I managed to ask in a weak voice, "Papa, why are you not taking us along?"

"There is no knowing what will befall Detroit. Here at least you are under the protection of the British." Papa's voice was sterner than ever. "While I cannot remain here, I will not let the British take my farm and all my crops and stock. They stole the land from my people in Ireland. They shall not have this land. You three children must see to the farm."

He turned to Jacques. "Son, you are too young to be made to take an oath. You will stay here and care for your sisters."

"But Papa, I can't stay here with two girls while you go and fight."

"Jacques, yours will be the harder part. By staying here on the island you will make a greater sacrifice than I will. I know I can trust you to do your duty."

Jacques turned away from Papa. I saw him steal a glance at Papa's musket that hangs on the wall of the cabin. He wanted to run off and fight but he was proud of Papa's trust. He looked back at Papa and nodded. When Papa asked Jacques to come with him so that he could tell him what must be done to care for Belle and the hogs and how the corn and potatoes were to be harvested, Jacques went along but he dragged his feet.

Later Papa showed Angelique how to do the accounts, for Jacques was too impatient to put one number after the other. "You must keep the house tidy," he told her, "and manage as best you can to put food upon the table. There may be times ahead when that will be hard to do. I count on you to help your sister with her lessons. Your fine penmanship and cleverness with sums will serve as an example to Mary."

Papa said nothing to me. I was afraid he thought me a child and useless. But just before bedtime he asked me to walk outside with him. The summer evening was pleasant. Apart from some candlelight down in the village homes, and a few lanterns at the fort, the island was dark. Overhead the stars poked holes of light in the black sky. The moon made a path of gold cobbles across the water of the great lake. Papa sighed. "I am sorrier than I can say to leave you children and this island. Nothing would make me go but the thought of betraying my country by taking an oath in support of its enemy."

"We will be very much alone," I said in a low voice.

"The Wests have promised to keep an eye on you."

I was indignant. "I will not have anything to do with the Wests. They have taken the British oath."

"Dr. West has his reasons. Remember,

Mary, how Pere Mercier said Sunday in church
that we must leave judgment to God, lest we be
judged ourselves. You will be living for many
months with people who support the British.
The British will rule this island. From all I have
seen, Captain Roberts is a fair man. I do not
think you have to be afraid, but you must not ask
for trouble. You have a temper, Mary, which
could make difficulties for you and your sister
and brother. Will you promise to guard what you
say?"

"Yes, Papa."

"I did not bring you out here to scold you,
Mary. I want to ask your help."

"Yes, Papa!" My heart leaped up.

"I would be less than honest if I did not tell
you there will be difficult days ahead for all of
us. What you can offer is the most important
thing of all. You have courage, Mary. Jacques is a
good lad but he is restless. He will always long to
be somewhere else. Angelique is becoming a
fine young woman, but she is a romantic. She
would live in a fairy palace and feed upon strawberries and cream. Life on a farm may prove too
harsh for her. That is why, young as you are, it is
you I depend upon. You love our island and our
farm just as it is. I believe you would do much to

keep it safe. You must help your brother and sister to hang on, to trust that a better time will come, and that I will return."

"Yes, Papa," I whispered. I was happier than I had ever been in my life.

Papa put a little packet into my hand. "Here is a gold five-dollar piece, Mary. Spend it only if there is a great need."

"How will I know, Papa?"

"You will know. Now go in to bed. I am going to stay out here a little longer." I saw Papa walking slowly out toward our fields and I knew he was saying good-bye to the farm. I watched until he disappeared into the darkness and I could see him no more.

CHAPTER

6

*P*APA LEFT FOR DETROIT the last week in
July. The day he left he waited on the beach
along with all the others who had refused to take
an oath of allegiance to the British. Lieutenant
Hanks and the American soldiers were there as
well. They stood at attention trying to make a
brave show of their rout from the island. Row-
boats would carry all those who were leaving to
the schooners docked in the bay. The schooners

were the *Mary* and the *Selina*, which the British had captured from the Americans.

Disagreements were forgotten. On this day there was only sadness as friend parted from friend. We feared for those who were leaving for Detroit. We worried the British forces would not rest until they had taken Detroit as they had captured Michilimackinac.

The Sinclairs were leaving. They had given their chickens to us. "Gavin will have plenty to do with what remains on the farm," Mr. Sinclair said. It was sad to see Gavin part from the Sinclairs. He would not show what he felt but stood apart holding all of his heartache inside.

Dr. West was assuring Papa that he would keep an eye on us. Emma and Elizabeth were staring at us with tears of sympathy. That kept me from showing how miserable I was. I would have died rather than let them see me cry. As unhappy as I was I could not help but notice how Emma glanced toward Jacques to be sure he was noticing how tender-hearted she was.

There were hundreds of Indians watching the departure along with a company of British soldiers. The soldiers, who kept to themselves, had been sent down from the fort to see that everyone boarded the ships. Pere Mercier was moving about comforting and blessing those who were departing.

The tenders that were to transport the passengers to the schooners came ashore. There was nothing left but to say farewell to Papa. He hugged us all in turn and then hugged us some more, not in turn, but just as we happened near him. The last hug was mine. As the boats rowed away we stood waving until everyone had boarded the schooners. Still we waited until one by one the sails were hoisted and the anchors hauled. Then we waved once again as the *Mary* and the *Selina* got under way. I was pleased that it had fallen to Papa to sail on the *Mary*, for it might be lucky that his ship had my name.

At the last minute Mrs. Sinclair had decided not to take her sack of new potatoes. She thrust them at Angelique. "Here, child, you will have a greater need for food." Now we looked for Jacques to help us carry them but he was nowhere to be seen. As we picked the sack up the string came loose and the potatoes rolled all over. I began to gather them up but Angelique was too mortified to help. Two British soldiers hurried to assist us. All the while they were

putting the potatoes back in the sack they were stealing looks at Angelique, who stood there like a princess letting me and the soldiers do all the work.

As I was putting the last potato in the sack, Jacques returned. He had left to talk with M. and Mme. Gauthier, who were packing their canoe for their trip across the lake. All the unhappiness at Papa's leaving was gone from Jacques's face. Instead he was excited. "The Gauthiers will go to Green Bay and Lake Winnebago and from there down the Fox River to Prairie du Chien and the Mississippi." He said all the names of the faraway places as if they tasted good in his mouth. "When I told them how much I wanted to see those places, they said they might take me with them next year. The portages are long and they could use another strong back to help carry the canoe and the packs."

"Jacques O'Shea!" Angelique was indignant. "Would you go off and leave us after Papa told you to take care of us?"

Jacques was taken aback by Angelique's angry voice, for she was seldom vexed.

Hastily Jacques said, "I only said they

offered to let me go with them. I did not say I would go. Anyhow, what were you doing being friendly with enemy soldiers?"

"I wasn't being friendly. You had deserted us and they came to help us."

"Stop it!" I said. "Papa's hardly gone and you're shouting at one another."

After that no word was said until we reached the farm. Jacques gathered wood for the fireplace while Angelique began to prepare dinner. I went to milk Belle. Sitting on the stool I rested my head against Belle's warm flank. I heard once that tears sour milk but I found out that is not true.

The cornbread was burned and the carrots nearly raw but no one complained. We kept trying not to look at the empty chair that stood at the head of the table. Finally I said, "Jacques, you must sit there."

Jacques did not move. He looked scared.

Angelique said, "Yes. That is your chair now."

Solemnly Jacques got up and slowly pulled out Papa's chair. He settled into it, but he looked so uncomfortable, so miserable, I giggled. Then Angelique began to laugh. In a minute we were

all three laughing so hard we started to cry. That was because our tears were so handy.

The first week after Papa left we all stayed close to the farm. Without him there was much more work to do. I had Belle and the chickens to care for. Jacques chopped wood for the winter and minded the hogs. Angelique took care of the house and the vegetable garden. We all hoed the cornfield.

One afternoon when Angelique had walked into the village with some eggs to sell and Jacques was in the forest cutting wood, the two British soldiers who had helped us with the potatoes came to the farm. They were on horseback. Next to having Papa back I'd rather have a horse than anything in the world.

I could tell they were the same soldiers because of how young they were. Their uniforms were too large for them. One of the soldier's tall hats slid down over his ears. I wondered that he did not roll a little cloth inside the hatband. I nearly gave him the hint before I remembered he was the enemy.

They got down from their horses and walked toward me. "We heard you had eggs for sale," said the soldier with the hat that was too big.

"Well, we do not," I told him. I would not sell eggs to the British. I hoped they all starved, although that was not likely since a lot of people on the island were selling them food.

"Is your sister here?" the other one asked. So that was why they had come.

"No she is not, and even if she were, she would not wish to see you." I stuck my chin out and looked as haughty as I could but it only caused the soldiers to smile. That made me really angry and I declared, "If you do not know it, this is private property."

"Yes, ma'am," the first soldier said. He noticed how I was staring at the horses. "Would you like to get up on my horse and take him for a little trot?" he asked, still smiling.

I wished I had said no right off. Instead it took me a second or two. But I said it.

CHAPTER

7

AUGUST WAS NEARLY over and we had
heard nothing from Papa. Tribes from all over—
the Sauk, the Winnebagoes, the Ottawas, and the
Chippewas—had come to the island to join the
Indians already here. They came with their
wives and children to celebrate the victory of the
British, over a thousand of them. Tents and wig-
wams were set up all along the beach, but you
might come upon the Indians anywhere. They
wandered over the island peering into windows

and looking over fences. Sometimes they came right into your house and sat down to watch you go about your work. The men entered the house with a strong step, but the women made no sound at all. At first we worried, for the Indians carried guns and tomahawks, but they were peaceful and gave no trouble to anyone.

In the evenings you could hear the Indians' drums and see their campfires down on the beach. Jacques often followed Gavin down to the camps. At first the Indians had laughed at Gavin in his white man's clothes. The laughter stopped when they heard his Indian name and the story of how he came to Michilimackinac. One elderly Indian said, "There are members of your clan living in L'Arbre Croche. You must come with us when we leave."

Gavin asked many questions about his clan, but he would not go with the Indians. "I have promised to remain here," he said, "and care for the Sinclairs' farm." Yet you could see he was longing to learn more about his people. There are islands in our hearts that no one can reach. My thoughts of my mother, whom I cannot remember, is such an island. I believe Gavin had many such islands in his heart.

Sometimes Jacques let me come along to the

camps with them. While Jacques and Gavin went in boldly, I stayed back. It was so noisy and there was so much going on. There were games of lacrosse and stones. There was wrestling and competitions with bow and arrow. The women in their deerskin shifts or calico dresses, many with beading and quill embroidery, prepared kettles of cornmeal porridge. The men nailed whitefish to planks and set the planks to roast at the edge of the campfire. Everywhere there were drums and singing and dancing.

In the warm August nights the men wore no shirts, only deerskin breeches. Their faces were painted in white and Prussian blue and bright yellow. The patterns they made were wonderful to see. There were faces divided into two halves with blue on one half and white on the other. One Indian had yellow circles around his brown eyes so that you felt two sunflowers were looking at you.

Around their necks were necklaces of beads and metal disks. Some had hats with feathers, some wore feathers in their hair. Some had fox tails affixed to their wrists and ankles. Many wore scalplocks so that should they be killed in a war, there would be a proper trophy for the enemy. Most impressive of all were the warriors, and there were only a few, who wore necklaces of grizzly bear claws. The grizzly bears were found in the West, which meant those warriors had traveled far and had fought a truly fierce battle for their trophy.

After the Indians had their dinner I would creep close to the camps to listen to their stories. Many of the stories were about the brave deeds of the warriors. Although I could not understand the Algonquin language of the Chippewa Indians, they were such good storytellers you could imagine what they were saying.

When they recited one of the many stories of how our island, Michilimackinac, the Great Turtle, came to be, Gavin told me what the storyteller was saying. Gitchi Manitou, the Great Spirit and maker of all things, created many different kinds of creatures to live in his lakes. The evil spirit, Mitchi Manitou, was jealous of all these wonderful creatures. When Gitchi Manitou made a turtle, the Evil Spirit told the turtle he must eat everything in the lake so that the work of the Great Spirit would be destroyed. The turtle ate the eggs of the fish. He ate the tiny shining minnows. He grew large. He ate the little fish: the perch and the blue gills. He grew larger. He ate all the *ticamang*, the whitefish.

Now his shell was many miles around and still the Evil Spirit whispered to him, "Eat, eat." He ate the muskellunge, a fish as large as a man. "Eat, eat," urged Mitchi Manitou. The great turtle swallowed the largest fish of all, the sturgeon. Upon seeing this, Gitchi Manitou became very angry with the turtle. "Turtle," he said, "you have eaten all the fish I have created. I will pile great rocks on your shell. I will plant many trees upon it. You will have to stay forever in one place. Never again will you be able to swallow all my fish." And that, he said, is how our island came to be. "It sits upon the shell of the great turtle, the *michilimackinac*."

After all the goods from the factory were given away to the Indians, Captain Roberts ordered the Indians to go to Fort Malden. We were alarmed, for we knew that Fort Malden was in Canada, close to Detroit, where Papa and all our friends were. Our worst fears were confirmed when Captain Roberts told the Indians that they were needed there because the British soldiers at Camp Malden would soon march on Detroit.

Once again the Indians urged Gavin to go with them. "The members of the Hawk Clan are all brave warriors. It is not right that you should be spoiled by the white man as they spoil their own children. You carry a book with you instead of a tomahawk. How will a book save you in a battle?"

Gavin shrugged, mumbling under his breath that if enough men read books there would be no battles. Still, I could see he was hurt by their words. When the time came for the Indians to leave for Fort Malden, Gavin stayed away from the beach. He would not go with them but he did not want to be shamed by their mocking of him.

Jacques and I, afraid for Papa and all of our friends in Detroit, watched the hundreds of canoes slip into the bay and head south on Lake Huron.

There was nothing for Jacques and Angelique and me to do but see to the farm. The corn had tasseled and would soon be ripe and ready to cut for fodder. The ears would be shucked and dried and seed corn saved out for next year's planting. There was little waste, for the chickens ate the corn silk and the hogs got the cobs. Bracken had to be cut for bedding for Belle. We dug potatoes to store in the root cellar. I even helped Jacques manure the empty fields.

Jacques took Belle across the island to M.

André's farm to spend the day with Jupiter. Jupiter was a bull. If Belle didn't have a calf about once a year she stopped giving milk. M. André had sold Belle to Papa when Belle was just a calf. To pay for Belle we had to promise M. André Belle's first four calves.

Angelique sent me out each day to pick blackberries for jam. I would coax Gavin to leave the work on his farm and go with me. Gavin always knew where the biggest and juiciest berries grew, but he wasn't much help with the picking. As soon as he was in the woods he would discover a bird with a white throat and a sweet song or a bird with a patch of yellow on its tail. He would follow it from tree to tree. If he wasn't tracking a bird he was sticking his nose into holes in trees to see what lived inside. One day he got stung and we got lucky.

"A bee tree!" he yelled, dancing around from the pain of the sting. He pointed to a dead tree he had been poking about in. "The tree is sure to be full of honey and wax."

"But how will we get it out without getting stung to death?"

"Find me some cloth and I'll show you."

While Gavin took out the tinderbox he always carried, I ducked behind some bushes.

Reaching under my skirt, I tore off a piece of petticoat. Gavin wrapped the piece of cloth around a handful of grass. He struck a piece of flint against the back of his knife until a spark caught the tinder. He held the tinder to the bundle of cloth and grass.

"You're burning my petticoat," I wailed.

He took the bundle, which was beginning to smoke, and held it in the hole of the tree where the bees had their nest. After a few minutes, he said, "Now, let's see what the bees have made for us." He reached inside and began to cut sections of wax comb dripping with honey. One by one he dropped the pieces into our empty berry pails. "Scrape off the bees," he said.

"They'll sting me."

"Not if you are quick. The smoke makes them sleepy."

Hastily I scraped the drowsy bees from their combs with a twig, licking my fingers to taste the sweet honey. When the pails were filled Gavin divided them, giving me much the larger part.

When she saw the honey Angelique hugged me. "*Merveilleux!* Honey to sweeten the cornbread and I can make an apple tart. There is wax for candles and for polish for the table and to seal the jam jars!" She wrapped the comb in cloth and hung it near the fireplace so the warm honey would drip out. Angelique was so pleased that when I told her a piece of my petticoat had been torn off by a blackberry briar, she only shook her head and said it could be patched. Relieved, I went out to feed the chickens.

I was gone a long time because two of the chickens were missing. I looked all over for them.

"Two of our chickens are lost," I told Angelique.

"The soldiers that helped with the potatoes came by asking to buy some of our chickens," Angelique said. "I sold two to them."

I was indignant. "How could you give our chickens to the enemy? Especially the Sinclairs' chickens."

"The soldiers were very polite and said there might be dances at the fort."

"You wouldn't go to their dances!"

Hastily Angelique said, "Of course not." But she wouldn't look at me.

The first hard frost came on the sixteenth of September. Jacques and Angelique and I had worked hard to harvest all of our crops. The cabin was fragrant with the herbs Angelique had dried: rosemary, thyme, mint, and sage. On the shelf was a row of jars filled with blackberry jam, each jar covered with a circle of cloth dipped in beeswax. The root cellar was filled with potatoes and turnips and squash. In the garden the carrots and parsnips were covered with straw. Even after the snow came we would be able to harvest them. Carrots and parsnips get sweeter the longer they are in the ground.

We peeled and sliced apples and put them out to dry in the sun, turning them every few hours. At night we covered them with a blanket so the dew would not moisten them. When they were dried we strung them together in festoons to hang on the rafters.

We knew Papa would be proud of us for working so hard. And all our hard work was there for us to see anytime we liked. We forgot to worry quite so much about Papa. Maybe we even forgot to pray hard enough, for at the end of September a canoe came with frightening news from Detroit.

CHAPTER

*T*HE TRAVELER and his canoe had been on the island for only a moment before everyone knew what had happened. Detroit had fallen! Jacques brought us the grim news. "The British army and hundreds of Indians marched on Fort Wayne. They demanded Detroit surrender. General Hull did not defend the fort nor did he surrender. He did not do anything! What do you think of that!"

And there was even worse news. "The British fired a cannon at the fort and the cannonball killed our Lieutenant Hanks!"

Lieutenant Hanks had commanded Fort Michilimackinac for more than a year. I had seen him many times riding through town on his horse. I felt terrible but all I wanted to hear about was Papa. "Jacques, what about our papa?"

Jacques was caught up in the telling of the story. "Let me finish. General Hull said he would surrender to the British if they promised that the people of Detroit sheltering inside the fort would be safe. So the British promised. Fort Wayne was surrendered. Right afterward the Indians who were fighting for the British took prisoners and people were killed. Many more would have been killed if it hadn't been for Tecumseh." I had heard of Tecumseh, the Shawnee chief and member of the Great Lynx Clan. He was a famous Indian warrior and a great leader. The British had even made him a brigadier general.

Jacques said, "Tecumseh watched over the Americans all night and saved their lives."

"Papa! What about Papa?"

The excitement died from Jacques's voice.

He shook his head. "The man doesn't know what happened to any of the people who left the island except Lieutenant Hanks."

At that Angelique and I burst into tears. I did not know how I could get through one more minute without knowing if Papa was safe. Yet there would be not only minutes, but hours and days and weeks before we knew. If the lake should freeze before a boat could come with a letter from Papa, it might be months.

Later that day Dr. and Mrs. West with Emma and Elizabeth brought us a ginger cake. Emma let Jacques know that she had had the greater part in the baking of the cake. Elizabeth was no help to her sister for she said, "Yes, but the first one you made burnt all up." Mrs. West must have guessed we had been too worried to eat, for she stirred about in our kitchen, putting the kettle on for tea and giving each of us thick slices of the cake, still warm from the oven.

Pere Mercier came as well. He had been fishing when the canoe arrived and had only just heard the news. His sad face looked sadder than ever and his black robe even blacker. He brought with him three large whitefish, which he had caught and cleaned. The shiny scales were scattered like pearls all over his black cassock. He said he was praying very hard for Papa. So between the ginger cake and the prayers we got through the day.

The night was harder. I could feel Angelique tossing and turning in our bed. Downstairs Jacques was moving about. No matter how I squinched them, my own eyes would not stay closed. "Angelique," I whispered, "are you awake?"

"Yes." I could tell from her voice she had been crying.

We wrapped ourselves in blankets and climbed down the ladder. Jacques had thrown more wood on the fire, so the room was nearly warm. I asked, "Angelique, isn't there a bit of that chocolate left?" Two years before, a trader had given a packet of chocolate to Papa in exchange for a wood box Papa had fashioned for him. Twice we had been allowed hot chocolate. It tasted better than anything in the world.

Jacques opened the cupboard and brought out the packet. "There's enough here for a cup for each of us."

Angelique mixed some milk and water together and heated it. I measured out the chocolate into three cups. Jacques cut the rest of the ginger cake. It wasn't because we were less worried that we fell asleep afterward; it was just that the cocoa had warmed the coldest places.

Every day we hoped for a letter from Papa, although we knew it would take many weeks for some trader to carry a letter all the way from Detroit. There was only more bad news. A family of Indians brought word that Fort Dearborn in Illinois had fallen to the British. I did not see how the American army would ever get their forts back so Papa could come home to us.

The weather grew colder. The wind, with no leaves on the trees to temper it, blew harder. In the morning the first rays of sun kindled the frost so that the whole farm sparkled. I helped Jacques fill our cart with logs of birch and oak and wild cherry. After we pulled the cart to our yard Jacques split the wood and I piled it as high as I could reach. Angelique piled it higher.

The acorns were plentiful and we gathered pailfuls for the hogs to eat. At the end of October Jacques butchered one of the hogs so we would have pork to salt away for the winter. Mr. MacNeil came from his blacksmith shop to help him, for a hog is a huge animal. The big iron kettle was brought out of the barn and a fire built beneath it. When the water began to boil I ran into the house. I didn't want to see what came next.

We heard the musket. I knew as soon as the hog was dead Jacques and Mr. MacNeil would lower it into the boiling water. The water would loosen the hog's hair so it could be scraped off. Then there would be the cutting up of the hog. It was such a bloody job that when the butchering was finished, and Mr. MacNeil had gone home, Angelique and I took turns pouring pails of water over Jacques.

In exchange for a share of the hog, Mr. MacNeil smoked the hams and bacon for us. It took several days. If you were anywhere near the MacNeils' you could smell the smoke from the applewood fire. My sister and I got out the meat grinder to make sausage. Angelique mixed in sage and savory from her herb garden. I plunged my hands into the mess and squished it all up. Together we filled the casings made from the hog's gut.

Since the liver and sweetbreads are best eaten fresh, and there was more than we could eat, I said, "Let's invite the Wests. They have been so good to us since Papa left." Jacques went to deliver the invitation. I set the table with Mama's linen cloth. The frost had killed the flowers, all but the witch hazel, which blossoms in October. Its blossoms are small, but their yellow flowers, like ragged stars, were pretty with our blue-and-white Delft dishes. Angelique used some of the lard from the pig for a plum tart. At last all was ready. The fire was chattering in the fireplace and the table was nicely set. Angelique was in her sprigged calico. I wore my good pinafore.

Dr. West brought a jug of cider for us. Mrs. West had a packet of maple sugar. As Elizabeth and Emma came in, Elizabeth held her skirts off the floor as though it might be dirty, which it certainly wasn't because I had swept it myself. Angelique overlooked Elizabeth's airs because Elizabeth often forgot who she thought she ought to be and became just like anyone else.

"Now isn't this a delightful gathering," Dr. West said. His cheerful voice set the tone of the evening.

"How nicely you are keeping your house, children," Mrs. West said. "I only wish Emma and Elizabeth had your clever hands." Emma looked embarrassed. Elizabeth looked pleased.

There was no reason Emma and Elizabeth could not scrub a floor or bake a loaf of bread as well as anyone, but Mrs. West thought such work unladylike. She taught her girls to think the same. Each day the youngest daughter of the tavern-keeper came to clean the Wests' house.

"I must say I have been met with nothing but courtesy in caring for the soldiers at the fort," Dr. West said. "Captain Roberts is a gentleman. His family owns a considerable estate in England."

Jacques said, "I do not believe just rich men should be officers. In England you pay for your commission so that any fool can lead men. In this country it is the best soldier who leads the men."

Dr. West smiled at Jacques' serious tone. "You have a point, my boy. Still, breeding counts for something."

"Maybe in hogs," Jacques said under his breath, so that I was the only one to hear him.

Elizabeth was saying, "What are you wearing to the dance, Angelique?"

"What dance?" I asked.

Elizabeth answered, "The officers at the fort are having a dance. They wish to know some of the young ladies in the town."

"You aren't going, are you, Angelique?" I asked, unable to believe she would dance with men who had sent Papa from our island.

Angelique blushed. "If I do, I do not see that it concerns you."

Dr. West looked from my angry face to Angelique's and quickly changed the subject. "Well, boy," he said to Jacques, "I see by the size of the stack of firewood you have out there that you are going to keep your sisters warm."

"Yes, sir. But if they have many such heated arguments as this one, there will be no need for firewood. My sisters' tempers will keep them warm."

Jacques' grin was so funny we could not keep up our anger and the whole table laughed, Emma the loudest. In no time we were once again pleasant to one another and the evening was pronounced a great success. Nothing was greater proof of it than Mrs. West sending her two girls in all of their finery to help Angelique and me with the washing up. Emma and I reached for the spoons and plates, leaving Elizabeth to dry all the pots and pans.

When the Wests were gone I asked Angelique, "Truly you wouldn't go and leap about with those terrible men in the fort?" I knew I should not have said more about the dance, but I could not hold my tongue. As Pere Mercier has read to us from the Bible, "The tongue can no man tame; it is an unruly evil full of deadly poison."

Angelique answered crossly, "I do not know why you say they are terrible men. They appear very gentlemanly to me. What harm can there be in it? Am I to do nothing for the rest of my life but redden my hands with scrubbing floors and ruin my complexion hoeing corn? Is my only pleasure in life to be watching Jacques bleed a pig and cut it up?" Her black curls were dancing with anger. She began to cry.

I felt terrible. I threw my arms around her and began to cry as well. "I'm sorry, truly I am. You can go to as many dances as you like. And you can wear my silver cross from Mama." The silver cross was the only thing of Mama's I possessed. "And you must be sure to have all the handsome officers for yourself so Elizabeth and Emma will have to dance with the ugly ones."

I still wasn't sure Angelique should have anything to do with the British soldiers. Still, God must not have been angry about Angelique going to the dance, for early in November a

French trader who had escaped from Detroit arrived by canoe and made his way to our farm. When he came I was home alone. Jacques was in the woods with Gavin hunting squirrels. Angelique was at the Wests' making over a dress to wear to the dance.

I heard a loud knock. There on the doorstep was a huge man wearing the wool *capot*, woven sash, and deerskin leggings of a *voyageur*. The lower part of his face was covered by a bushy black beard. The rest of his face was hidden by a thatch of long, straggly, greasy hair. Somewhere in the tangle of beard and hair two black shoe-button eyes stared down at me. "Mademoiselle O'Shea?" he asked, leaving off half the letters of our name as the French do. "I have news for you of your papa."

"Is he alive?"

"*Oui*, mademoiselle. He has the good health. Here is a letter from him which he bade me deliver."

I grabbed the letter and forgetting myself entirely I threw my arms around the *voyageur*. He smelled of wood smoke and tobacco. I felt a large hand pat my head. Just at that moment, a startled Jacques walked into the house with Gavin. "Papa's safe!" I cried.

Eagerly we read his letter:

My dearest children,

I only hope this will reach you before you hear the sorry news about Detroit. It is true we lost Fort Wayne but there was nothing else General Hull could have done. Had he not surrendered, the people of the city would have been sacrificed. As it was many were killed or taken prisoner. The hero of the day was Tecumseh. Though he led the Indians against us, when we surrendered he risked much to protect us. All night he patrolled outside the stockade. Over and over he ordered away those who would climb over the pickets to harm the people who had come there for protection.

I am sorry to have to tell you that the Sinclair family were carried away as prisoners to the Indian village of L'Arbre Croche. They will be held there as hostages until money is paid for their return. Pass this news on to Gavin. Tell him we must hope for the best.

I am on my way to join General Winchester. We have every expectation of taking Detroit back. American troops are even now making their way from the East.

I carry all of you in my heart and only pray

I have done the right thing to fight for my country against those who long have threatened our liberty. Remember me in your prayers.

Your loving Papa

We read the letter over and over. When Angelique came we read it again. At last we began to remember our manners and to press upon M. LeGrande, the *voyageur,* food and drink. Though he ate nearly everything in the house it gave us the greatest pleasure to sit across the table from him and watch him do it. Just seeing him made us feel closer to Papa.

M. LeGrande had to be off early in the morning for he was on his way west to bring goods to the traders. We urged him to spend the night with us, which he readily agreed to do. Angelique offered him a basin and some warm water with which to wash, but he said he had washed already that month and there was no further need.

In our joy at learning of Papa's safety we had not thought of how Gavin must be feeling. Now we saw how agitated he was. Again and again he asked M. LeGrande about L'Arbre Croche, where the Sinclair family had been taken as prisoners. L'Arbre Croche was the home of the

Ottawa. The one thing Gavin knew about himself was that his parents had been Ottawa and that some of his tribe might be there. I thought that was why he had so many questions. Then he asked, "How long would it take to go there by canoe?"

"A day and a half, perhaps two days. The paddling is not so easy. This time of year the *tempêtes de l'automne*, the storms of autumn, come over the lake without warning."

While I lay in bed I could hear Jacques and Gavin coaxing from M. LeGrande tales of his adventures with the traders. Even after they were quiet I could not sleep, for Gavin's many questions about L'Arbre Croche buzzed through my head like a swarm of stinging wasps.

CHAPTER

9

ALTHOUGH ANGELIQUE and I were down the ladder before the sun was up, M. LeGrande had already taken his leave. Jacques and Gavin had gone to see him off. When they returned, Gavin was carrying a small bundle carefully wrapped in a piece of calico. Together they went off into the woods saying they were after firewood, but when they returned they brought no wood with them. Instead Jacques announced, "Gavin and I are going to L'Arbre Croche in my canoe."

I sank down upon the nearest chair, speechless.

"You cannot think of risking your lives in such a way!" Angelique cried. "Suppose the Indians keep you as well?"

Gavin was determined. "I will not see Mama and Papa in such trouble and do nothing," he said. "L'Arbre Croche is where my clan is. They must be told of the Sinclairs' kindness to me. They must learn that Mr. Sinclair saved my life."

Jacques turned to me. "Mary, give me the gold piece Papa gave to you. We will give it to the Indians so they will set the Sinclairs free."

"I won't give you the money! You will drown!" All I could think of was M. LeGrande's description of the fierce autumn storms. "You cannot go!"

"We mean to go whether you give me the money or not. Only if you decide not to, it will be much harder to ransom the Sinclairs."

What he meant was that it would be more dangerous. I tried to think what Papa would want me to do.

"I owe my life to the Sinclairs," Gavin said.

"I would gladly give it for their safety."

That decided me. There was nothing but to trust that Jacques and Gavin would be careful. I unwrapped the five-dollar gold piece and handed it to Jacques.

"I only hope it will be enough," Jacques said.

I thought of the Sinclairs separated from all of their friends. Winter would be coming on and they would have no shelter but an Indian wigwam. I truly didn't want to, but before I could stop myself I unfastened Mama's silver cross from around my neck and handed it to Gavin. Gavin wouldn't take it, but Jacques said they must and put it in his pocket. I was shocked at what I had done. Good deeds must come from the heart. They cannot come from the head. For if I had thought about it I would never have parted with the silver cross. My only comfort at losing it was that it might help to keep them safe on their journey.

All that day Jacques and Gavin worked on the canoe. It was made of white birch stretched upon a frame of split cedar and sewn together with the roots of hemlock trees. To make it sound for the hard trip to L'Arbre Croche they spread a new coat of resin from the pine trees over the bark. I looked with misgiving at the small canoe. It was meant for calm and shallow waters. It was not meant for water so deep there was no seeing to the bottom of it, nor for storm waves as high as a house.

Jacques and Gavin left secretly at night, for they worried that the British would not approve such a rescue mission. The British would not wish restored to the island those who had opposed them. Our only hope was that once the Sinclairs were returned they would not be sent away. With many tears Angelique and I bid Jacques and Gavin farewell. We did not dare risk following them all the way to the beach, so there was no one to watch them set forth on the dark waters.

They were gone only a few hours when a cold November fog spread over the lake. It was as though all the clouds in the heavens had been let down. The island and the lakes as far as you could see were muffled in veil after veil of fog. How were Jacques and Gavin ever to find their way?

Since Angelique and I were afraid to confide in even our closest friends, we had no one to share our worries. For three nights we did not sleep. Apart from tending to Belle, and the feeding of the pigs and chickens, no work was done on the farm. We could only wait and pray.

On the fourth night we had just put out the candles and were making ready for bed and for another sleepless night when the door was pushed open. Jacques and the Sinclairs hurried into the cabin. They were as damp and bedraggled as three wet chickens. Mr. Sinclair's jacket lacked a sleeve. Mrs. Sinclair's bonnet was front to back. They were shivering and rushed to warm themselves at the remains of our fire.

We were so relieved to see them safe we could do nothing but embrace them and rejoice over their deliverance. We rushed to get blankets and dry clothes for them. The teakettle was set to boil and food brought out. It was several minutes before I thought to ask, "Where is Gavin?"

At that Mrs. Sinclair broke into tears. "What is it?" My heart forgot to beat, for to tell the truth I am very fond of Gavin.

"He is gone from us forever," Mrs. Sinclair sobbed.

"Is he drowned?" Angelique was as frightened as I.

Mr. Sinclair was comforting his wife. "Gavin is safe, but he has decided to stay at L'Arbre Croche for a while."

"He will never come back to us," Mrs. Sinclair moaned.

"Now, Charlotte, we must hope that one day he will return."

Though I wished Gavin were in the room with the rest of us, his safety let my heart resume its work.

After Mrs. Sinclair had calmed herself and Angelique had poured the tea and I had built up the fire, Jacques told us the whole story.

"We nearly lost our way in the fog but we followed the shore. Luckily there were Indian campfires along the way to guide us. In the fog we could still make out the fires but the lookouts could not see us.

"We arrived near L'Arbre Croche the second day. We stayed offshore until dark. By then the fog had lifted. Our plan was to beach our canoe a mile or two from L'Arbre Croche and make our way to the Ottawa camp. From there we would scout out where the Sinclairs were being held. Instead an Indian lookout spotted us. We were met with a dozen canoes. Gavin managed to convince the Ottawa we were there on a friendly mission to ransom the Sinclairs. They escorted our canoe to the camp where the chief was waiting for us.

"The chief was civil enough but we could see he was suspicious of Gavin. Gavin was dressed in white man's clothes and spoke white man's language as well as the Indian language. I can tell you it was frightening to see hundreds of unfriendly faces staring at us from around their campfires. That was when Gavin brought out that sacred bundle thing he had when the Sinclairs found him. He gave it to the chief and told the chief how his mother and father had been drowned on their way to L'Arbre Croche.

"As he was telling the story the chief looked more and more astonished. All the Indians gathered around to listen. When Gavin finished they began to talk with one another and with the chief. They passed around the sacred bundle, the *pitchkosan*, that Gavin had brought. There was a lot of shouting and jumping around. I thought they were going to do away with us right then and there. Instead they fell all over Gavin, patting him and slapping him on the back. It turned out that his father had been a chief. It was thought that Gavin had been drowned with the rest of his family. They couldn't do enough for us. They led out the Sinclairs at once."

Mr. Sinclair said, "We couldn't believe our eyes when we saw Gavin and Jacques. At first we thought that they had been taken prisoner as well. Gavin explained they were there to ransom us. He told the chief that I had saved him from drowning and Mrs. Sinclair and I had raised him. Jacques showed the chief the five-dollar gold piece but the chief waved it away. He said Gavin was the son of one of their chiefs. Since I had saved him, my wife and I were free to go at once. In fact he made a long speech of apology for taking us."

"Here's the five-dollar gold piece," Jacques said. "And here is Mama's silver cross."

At this Mrs. Sinclair's velvet eyes filled with tears. "How kind you all were to be so generous in rescuing us. How can we ever thank you?"

"Indeed," Mr. Sinclair said. "Winter was coming on and we should have been very miserable. I believe you saved our lives." He clasped Jacques on the shoulder and turned his face so that we should not see him brush away a tear.

"But why did Gavin not come back?" I asked.

Mr. Sinclair's voice was solemn. There must not have been much food at the Indian camp, for his clothes hung upon him and his cheeks were sunken. "You can imagine what it meant to Gavin to discover who he was and to find the people to whom he belongs."

"He belongs to us," Mrs. Sinclair cried. For the first time I noticed that under her bonnet her hair was gray. Her hands as they lay in her lap trembled so that she had to clasp them together.

"Of course he belongs to us, my dear, but he also belongs to his people. He wants to get to know them. He wants to understand more of their life and their customs. I am sure he will return to us one day."

Mrs. Sinclair only shook her head. "I would rather have frozen to death in the Indian camp than lose Gavin. And what will become of all the schooling he has had?"

"That will not be wasted," Mr. Sinclair said. "This may be a sad day for us, but for his people it may prove a blessing."

I did not see how that could be, but I was happy that Gavin had learned who he was. As kind as the Sinclairs had been to him he must many times have wondered about his real mama and papa. Even though I knew who my mama was, I had often wished I could have known her as most children know their mothers.

Still, I worried that I would never see Gavin

again. Or even worse. Although nothing was said, we all knew the Ottawa were on the side of the British. When the American soldiers came back to free our island, the Ottawa would surely be summoned from L'Arbre Croche to fight against them. On whose side would Gavin fight?

There was much discussion about what the Sinclairs should do. It would be impossible for them to go unnoticed on such a small island, yet there was no place else for them. Mr. Sinclair decided. "I must report to the fort tomorrow. I will throw myself upon the mercy of Captain Roberts. I cannot believe he will send us away."

Indeed, Mr. Sinclair was right. When the whole story was told of what the Sinclairs had been through and when it was learned that Indians, friendly to the British, had released the Sinclairs, they were given leave to return to their farm. The whole island came to hear their story and to bring them provisions to help them through the winter.

When Pere Mercier learned that his finest pupil had remained with his people at L'Arbre Croche, he looked thoughtful. "It is not the way I would have chosen for him," he said, "but we must believe it is for the best." With that, although it was not much, I had to be content.

10

ON THE FIRST DAY of December the snow began to fall. It fell until it made a new world. Paths and fences were buried. Nothing looked the same. The snow covered the empty brown earth like a clean white cloth spread over a worn table. The air, sulky in November, turned as brittle as glass. Angelique and Jacques and I went outside and jumped from the top of the roof onto a snowdrift twice as high as we were. Jacques hammered some boards together and we slid down the hill. For once Angelique didn't think about being a lady but let the wind toss her black curls and redden her cheeks.

At night we stood at the window and watched the snow cover over all the traces of the fun we had. It was like erasing the writing on a piece of paper so that you might start fresh the next day. It was only when the snow wouldn't stop that we began to worry.

Jacques shoveled snow against the walls of Belle's shed to keep in the warmth from her body. Angelique kept a pot of snow melting over the fire, for the walk to the spring was a cold one. In the vegetable garden I dug under the snow and pushed aside the straw to pull up carrots and parsnips cold as chips of ice. Jacques put on snowshoes to take the milk and cream and eggs into town to sell. Once he slipped and broke six precious eggs so that he came home looking like an omelet.

Dr. West stopped by to be sure all was well. His face was pinched and drawn from staying up many nights. Besides his duties at the fort, he was caring for families suffering from whooping cough. The disease was everywhere.

"Things are not going well at the fort," he said. "The soldiers complain they have no winter clothes and there are none to be had on the island. Out of pity Captain Roberts has issued his men blankets to make into coats, but he is put out by those soldiers who think too much of their whiskey and too little of their duty." He shook his head and said sadly, "The captain himself is not well. I should not be surprised to see him relieved of his command before long."

"Is there any talk at the fort of a Christmas dance?" Angelique asked. She and Elizabeth still gossiped over the dance they had attended in the fall.

Dr. West shook his head. "I am afraid a dance is the last thing they think of there. It will be all they can do this winter to feed their men. That is one of the reasons I have come here today. They would take it as a kindness at the fort if you would sell your milk and eggs to them. Soon the lake will freeze and the supply ships will be unable to get here. Stores at the fort are low. I am afraid some of the men may go hungry."

Since the day Angelique had sold off two of our chickens to the soldiers we had given nothing more to the fort. I said, "Papa may even now be fighting the British. Why should we care if they are hungry?"

"Now they ask politely if you will sell to

them and they are prepared to pay." Dr. West's voice became grim. "If you refuse they may come and take what they wish and give you nothing for it but trouble."

Jacques reached with his eyes for Papa's musket, which hung on the wall. "Let them try."

Dr. West frowned. "The Lord watched over you, Jacques, when you did a foolish thing. Even *His* patience would be tried if you planned to take on an entire regiment." Dr. West had not forgiven Jacques for risking his life to bring back the Sinclairs. Secretly he thought Jacques and Gavin brave, but he had promised Papa to keep us safe. Had something happened to Jacques, Dr. West would never have forgiven himself.

I had already heard from the townspeople how some of the British soldiers had taken what they needed from them, paying little for it. I believed Dr. West when he said they might do the same to us. I gave him as hard a look as I could manage. "Would they pay double what we get in town?" I asked. I thought if I could get the British to pay twice what everything was worth it would be a way of beating them. Besides, we needed the money. Angelique's fingers poked out of her wool mitts. Jacques, like the soldiers, had no jacket.

Mr. West looked thoughtful. "They have more money than supplies." Then for the first time he smiled. "I am sure, Mary, you will not fail to get the better of them."

The next day I hurried to the fort. The sentry stood at the North Sally Port stamping his boots. He wore one of the jackets made from a trading blanket. It was white with red and yellow stripes. For a little warmth he had wrapped his legs with rags. With his red nose and with icicles hanging from his beard he looked so miserable standing there I almost felt sorry for him. When I insisted upon seeing Captain Roberts the sentry only laughed at me. "Captain Roberts has a fort to take care of. He has no time for children."

"I am not a child. I am here on business. I understand he is in want of eggs and milk and I have some to sell."

At that the sentry paid me serious attention. "I'll call the quartermaster, miss. He would be the one in charge of supplies for the fort. We would welcome the taste of a fresh egg and a swallow of milk. Indeed we would. We have nothing to eat but salt pork with rice soup and coffee."

"You must call Captain Roberts, for I won't talk with anyone else." Just then the entrance to the fort opened and two officers in fine red jackets gauded up with much gold braid rode out on their handsome horses. Seeing the sentry talking with me, the first officer said, "Wilson, it is not part of your duty to pass the time of day with young girls."

The sentry stood at attention, his face scarlet. "No, sir. This girl wanted to talk with the captain, sir. She has provisions to sell to the fort."

At that the other officer, who wore a plume in his tall hat, looked down at me. "Well, what have you to sell, young lady? I am Captain Roberts."

He looked very grand sitting on his horse. But to me he was the man who had captured our island and made Papa go away. I did not want to sell to him, so I asked three times as much as milk and eggs would bring in town, nine cents a dozen for the eggs alone.

"You ask a great deal, but we are in want of provisions and I must take what I can find. Wilson, call the quartermaster and tell him that I have accepted this young lady's offer." He actually saluted me and rode off.

The sentry shrugged. "Most likely your eggs and milk will find their way to the officers' table and not to ours." Then he went to find the quartermaster.

At home I told my story in one gulp.

"You asked for Captain Roberts!" Jacques said.

"He will pay us all that money!" Angelique could not believe it.

I went each day to the fort with jugs of milk and cream and a basket of eggs. I had to carry everything well wrapped so that the eggs and milk would not freeze on the way. Each day I returned with money that soon bought Jacques a blanket which Angelique fashioned into a jacket. Angelique and I bought wool. We pretended we were knitting something for ourselves. Secretly Angelique was knitting me a cap for New Year's, when it was the custom to exchange gifts. I was knitting her mitts. Together we took turns working on a scarf for Jacques. We kept the scarf hidden when he was in the house. For his part Jacques was making something in the stable and would not tell us what it was.

On the way to church Christmas Day it was snowing so hard we had to hang on to one another so as not to be caught in the white whirlwind. At St. Anne's there was a great stamping and brushing off of snow. Several soldiers had come from the fort. Their guns were neatly stacked at the door, for Pere Mercier would not have arms in St. Anne's.

The church was fragrant with the smell of the pine and hemlock branches that decorated the altar. All the candles were lit for the High Mass. Pere Mercier wore a robe embroidered in gold. Underneath, I saw, he had on his coat buttoned up to his chin, for there was no heat in the church. I envied the tin of hot coals the Wests had brought to warm their feet. My own feet and hands were numb with cold.

During the service Angelique whispered that the French Christmas carol we were singing was one Mama used to sing and I saw a tear slip down her cheek.

After the service Pere Mercier asked the Sinclairs if anything had been heard of Gavin. The Sinclairs were not Catholic but St. Anne's was the only church on the island. On Christmas Day the Protestant families came to St. Anne's closing their eyes to "all the mysterious hocus-pocus."

Pere Mercier said, "I want to believe Gavin will come back to us."

The Sinclairs could say nothing to encourage Pere Mercier for two canoes of Indians from

L'Arbre Croche had stopped at our island on the way to their winter hunting grounds at Sault Sainte Marie. They carried a letter to the Sinclairs from Gavin.

Dear Mr. and Mrs. Sinclair,

> *I must stay on here for some time. When I was a child you taught me many things. Now my people wish to teach me and I wish to learn from them. I send my compliments to the two of you whom I hold in the greatest esteem.*

> *I remain your dutiful friend,*

> *White Hawk*

The Sinclairs were glad to hear that Gavin was well, but the letter made them sad. Gavin's words were polite but colder than winter. He had always called them Mama and Papa. Now they were Mr. and Mrs. Sinclair. The letter was not signed "Gavin," but "White Hawk." And though I looked hard at the letter, I could find no word of greeting for Jacques or for myself.

When he heard about the letter Pere Mercier could only shake his head. To cheer him Jacques said that soon the lake would be frozen over. That meant he and Pere Mercier would be able to fish through the ice. Even that prospect did nothing to take away the priest's sadness for he missed his lessons with Gavin. Though I could say little of my own feelings, I missed Gavin as well.

Both the Sinclairs and the Wests had kindly invited us to spend Christmas Day with them but we declined. We wished to be in our own home where Papa seemed closer to us. Although we lost pennies in the doing of it, Angelique used six eggs to make Mama's recipe for *les crêpes* for our Christmas breakfast. She baked a fancy bread with bits of dried apple and pear worked into it. We even kept back from the fort some cream to make butter. I gave Belle an extra portion of hay. The pigs got a bit of buttermilk with their slops.

On New Year's Day, which Angelique called *le Jour de l'An*, we truly missed Papa. He had kept Mama's French custom of giving a benediction to each one of us on the first morning of the new year. After our blessings he would have a gift for each of us. Still, we were not forgotten. The Sinclairs sent us a featherbed. Mrs. Sinclair plucked their geese three times a year, so her featherbeds were thick and cozy with down. The Wests sent enough calico for two dresses.

Angelique was much pleased with the mitts I had knitted. She seemed not to notice the dropped stitches and knotted wool. My cap from her had a jaunty tassel on the top. Jacques declared his scarf was so long that one end of it could remain at home while the other accompanied him into town. His gift to us, which he brought in from its hiding place in the stable, was a great wooden bowl hollowed out from the bole of a maple tree. He had rubbed and rubbed it with beeswax until the grain of the wood shone.

The week that followed New Year's was so cold that the snow squeaked under my feet when I went to the cow shed. Because we had to use our firewood sparingly, the house was nearly as cold as the outdoors. When we talked little puffs came out of our mouths so that our words had a shape. Even the Sinclairs' featherbed could not keep Angelique and me warm. We scrambled down from the loft to curl up like cats in front of the fire.

The lakes froze over. Now we knew we would have no further word from Papa until the spring and our hope died a little. Jacques and Pere Mercier chopped holes in the frozen lake, but the fish were stubborn and would not bite.

In the henhouse, the chickens, peevish at being shut up, began pecking at one another. It was the same with us. Closed into the house day after day, I am sorry to say our tempers grew short. Angelique scolded Jacques for dragging in firewood after she had just swept the floor. Jacques complained that Angelique would cook nothing but turnips one day and carrots the next. Jacques and Angelique were both angry with me because I spent so much time in the woods.

I had learned from Gavin how to track animals. The marks of a vole's tiny paws and trailing tail, or the baby hand imprints of a raccoon's feet were like secret messages written in the snow. One day I discovered wolf tracks—a heart-shaped pad and four toes. I decided the wolf must have wandered across the ice from the mainland.

I followed the tracks all afternoon half hoping to see the wolf, half afraid of meeting it. The snow clung in clumps and drifts on the tree branches. As I walked along I yanked the branches sending down a fall of snow. For a while the wolf was on the trail of a beaver. You could see it was a beaver by its snowshoe tracks and the flat drag of its tail. The beaver's trail stopped at a pond. It must have escaped the wolf by slipping away into the water. Just as the sun was going down I happened to look over my shoulder. There was the wolf with its white muzzle and belly and its gray-brown coat frosted with snow. It had stopped and was staring at me with its yellow slanted eyes.

It stood its ground, its teeth bared. After a moment that seemed to last forever, the wolf turned and loped off into the woods. I had been going in a circle. I thought I was tracking the wolf and all the time the wolf was following me! With darkness at my heels I hurried home and never said a word to anyone. I knew that if Jacques found out he would hunt the wolf down and shoot it.

February brought the coldest day of the winter. It started out with a cloud of fog lowering over the island hiding all the trees. By the middle of the morning the sun began to shine through the cloud. When the fog disappeared it left a miracle behind. On all the trees bits of moisture were frozen into crystal. Every tree on the island glittered with diamonds of hoarfrost. We were so dazzled that for that whole day we had not a cross word to say to one another.

I often looked for the wolf's tracks but never again found them. All winter long it was my favorite secret.

CHAPTER

11

*D*URING ALL those long winter days spring was our hope. But the spring of 1813 arrived slowly, one bird at a time. First the gulls came flying back to gather on the rocks and shout at one another. Soon I heard the raspy calls of the red-winged blackbirds and the rackety sound of the kingfisher as it flew low over the melting ice, hungry for minnows. The birds that were so faithful all winter, the chickadees and jays, counted for nothing against the excitement of the returning birds.

One day the spring beauties and trailing arbutus were blooming in the woods. The next the lilac bush Mama had planted in our yard was flowering. In between those few weeks there seemed to be a year of work. We turned the chickens out into the yard and Belle out to pasture with her new calf who would soon go to M. André. If we took the calf too soon, Belle would moo in the most pitiable way. I was anxious for the time when Belle could keep her calves.

The sows and the boar began digging for roots and buried acorns. Jacques cleaned the cow shed out. We drew straws to see who would have to clean the henhouse, which is the dirtiest job in the world. It was me. I wrapped my hair in a rag and put a clothespin on my nose. Afterward it took two trips to the spring to fill the tub with water so I could have a decent bath.

The Sinclairs lent Jacques their plow and their horses. As he plowed the furrows in which we would plant our corn and potatoes, Angelique and I picked up the stones the plow turned up and made a pile of them. Papa was an expert stonemason. He had put together Belle's shed from a stone pile. I think we believed if we just gathered up enough stones, he would be sure to appear to make something new.

My favorite job was planting the vegetable garden. The day I began the earth was soft and warm. A white-throated sparrow sang overhead. A great toad heaved up through the dirt where it had lain buried all winter. Warmed by the sun it hopped about beside me like a tiny bloated dog. In no time the green flags of seedlings told us we had won the battle of winter.

Although we had not heard from Papa, with the lake open we began once again to hope for good news. Instead, we had to watch as Captain Roberts assembled hundreds of Indians on the island. Pledged to fight for the British, they were rallying on Michilimackinac before leaving to defend Fort Wayne in Detroit. We were sure the American soldiers meant to retake it, and that Papa would be with them. The Indians stayed on the island several days, and we rejoiced each day they stayed for that was one more day they would not trouble Papa.

Some of the Indians came from L'Arbre Croche, so we hoped to hear about Gavin. We did not expect to see Gavin himself, for we could not believe Gavin would join the Indians to fight the Americans.

On a bright June day when Jacques and I were scraping the tent caterpillars from the apple trees an Indian walked up the path toward us. It was not until he was close that we saw it was Gavin. We hadn't recognized him in his Indian clothes.

We were so pleased to see him, neither of us stopped to think of what he was doing on the island. We just guessed he had come back to the Sinclairs. Flustered and trying to hide my great pleasure, I said, "How glad the Sinclairs must be to have you back, Gavin." It was all I could do not to clasp his hand.

He answered, "You must call me White Hawk now." He was silent for a moment. "I have not seen the Sinclairs and I do not know if I will."

I was shocked. "Why don't you want to see them?"

"I do want to see them. I am only afraid they will not want to see me."

"Why ever would they not wish to see you?" Jacques asked.

Gavin looked at the ground. He mumbled, "I am here with my tribe. We go south to join the British army."

Jacques was furious. "You can't do that. You would be our enemy."

Gavin said in a loud voice, "I will never be your enemy."

I was as angry as Jacques. "What do you call yourself then when you go to wage war against us?"

"You must understand. All these months that I have been with my people, they have told me how the American government has taken their land and will take more. President Jefferson wished all the Indians to settle west of the Mississippi. Our chiefs have been deceived into parting with fifty million acres. The British promise to leave our land alone."

"You are very foolish if you believe the British," Jacques said. "They are as eager to take land as the Americans. What about the three thousand Acadians in Canada? All their land was taken from them and the British transported them a thousand miles from Canada."

Gavin kicked at a stone. "The Acadians were French."

"If the British can do such things to the French they can just as well do them to the Indians," said Jacques. In a blustery voice he added, "You have joined the British to fight Papa and we will have nothing more to do with you. And if you want my opinion, you look silly in those clothes."

I thought Gavin would be very angry. Instead he looked sad. With no further word he turned away from us and started down the path. I could not let him go with nothing but wrathful words to remember. Before I knew what I was doing I ran after him. "Gavin, wait for me. Let me walk with you. I think you look very grand in your Indian clothes. You look . . ." I tried to think of a word. "You look royal."

Gavin smiled bitterly. "In a way I am royal. I have learned my uncle is the chief of my clan. He has no sons and the clan wishes me to become its chief one day. My uncle prepares me for this."

"But must you fight?"

"I must learn to be a warrior. A chief must be able to protect his people."

Gavin was walking so fast toward the town I was running to keep up with him. "The Sinclairs will be unhappy if you do not see them."

"Look how your brother treated me. The Sinclairs will be just as angry."

I saw that I could not change his mind and turned away. I had gone only a short distance when I came to the path that led to the Sinclairs' farm. I took it. I didn't know what I would say for I was afraid of telling the Sinclairs the truth. How would they feel to learn that Gavin, whom they looked upon as their son, would be fighting with the British? He would be on the side of the same Indians who had carried them away from Detroit.

When I reached their cabin I found the Sinclairs pruning their grapevines. This gave me courage. Four years out of five a killing frost came to the island before the Sinclairs' grapes were ripe. Still they tended their vines for that one year when they would be able to harvest the grapes. The Sinclairs were not easily disappointed.

"Mary," Mrs. Sinclair called, "I am pleased to see you. Would you ask Angelique if I might have a slip of her rosemary plant? Ours died in the winter." As I came closer she said, "Why, child, what is it?"

I blurted everything out at once. "Gavin is here on the island and he's dressed in Indian clothes because he is going to be a chief and he's joined the British." My words were worse than any killing frost. The Sinclairs reached for one another as though they needed to hold each other up after my terrible blow.

Mr. Sinclair said, "Why is it left to you,

Mary, to tell us this? Why has not Gavin come to see us?"

"He is afraid you will be angry with him. He told Jacques and Jacques quarreled with him."

"We cannot pretend to be happy, but Gavin is still our son," Mrs. Sinclair said.

Mr. Sinclair shook his head. "I am not so sure."

"Mary, you must show us where he is. I for one am going to him." Mrs. Sinclair turned to her husband. "My dear, will you not come with Mary and me?"

I saw that Mr. Sinclair was only waiting to have the matter taken out of his hands for he followed us at once.

When we reached the Indian encampment Mr. Sinclair sent me on alone. "It is better if you bring him here. His people might wonder at his meeting with us. We are known to be unfriendly to the British cause."

The Indians paid me little attention for children were often attracted to their camp to watch them. I had to ask twice but at last I found Gavin. As soon as he saw me he hurried toward me. "Why have you followed me?"

"The Sinclairs are here. They wish to see you."

"Are they very angry?" he asked, looking more like a little boy than an Indian chief. He followed me to the grove of hemlocks where the Sinclairs were waiting. Mrs. Sinclair all but fell upon Gavin. Even Mr. Sinclair could not help putting an arm about Gavin's shoulder.

"Mama, Papa," Gavin said, forgetting that lately he had called them Mr. and Mrs. Sinclair. "The path I take has nothing to do with you. I have no wish to hurt you."

"We know that, Gavin," Mrs. Sinclair said. "You and Jacques risked your lives to bring us back here. We only wish you would stay on the island with us."

"Consider, Gavin, what you are throwing away," Mr. Sinclair pleaded. "You have the beginnings of a fine education. Surely you could do more for your people if you brought your learning to the task."

"There are many kinds of learning, Papa," Gavin said. "If I am to help my people, I must live with them to understand them. No book can teach me what they can teach me. I promise, though, not to forget my books, and someday I will take them up again."

With that the Sinclairs had to be satisfied. After Gavin had answered many questions about his life at L'Arbre Croche and after many promises that he would be careful should he find himself in a battle, the Sinclairs reluctantly said good-bye.

I was standing apart from the Sinclairs. As Gavin left us he came to me and said softly, "I am glad you were such a busybody." He removed a necklace of blue-and-white beads from around his neck and, slipping it over my head, hurried away. Before I reached our cabin I put the necklace in my pocket so Jacques would not see it. That night I slipped it under my pillow, knowing I would have to rescue it on the days Angelique shook out our bedclothes.

Within a week of our meeting with Gavin the Indians were gone from the island. If there was fighting between the British and the Americans, I had not only Papa to worry about, but Gavin as well. No matter which side won, there would be something to trouble me. When I said my prayers I blessed both Papa and Gavin. God would have to decide what to do.

With no news of Papa the summer was a long one with few sunny days. The rain helped the corn and potatoes grow but it dampened our spirits. It crept into the chinks of the cabin making the bread moldy and the sheets clammy. There was great relief when the first cool breezes of September arrived.

In the fall Captain Roberts was so ill he was relieved of his duty and a Captain Richard Bullock was made commander of the fort. Few liked him, for he was a rough man. We believed it was his doing that payments for the food we sold the fort, not only milk and eggs but potatoes and corn as well, were cut to almost nothing. When Jacques complained the quartermaster said he had his instructions from Captain Bullock. "If you do not wish to sell to the fort at the price the captain names, he will send someone to take what they like from your farm with no payment at all."

While we were preparing for our second winter we heard astonishing news. A trader arrived one afternoon to announce that the British navy had been soundly defeated by the Americans under Captain Oliver Hazard Perry. We could see Captain Bullock sulking over this British defeat. The British navy was no longer able to protect his fort. We Americans on the island celebrated the good news. Captain Perry was our hero. His brave declaration, "We have met the enemy and they are ours," was repeated over and over.

Two weeks later a boat arrived with secret letters from Detroit. Angelique, who had been in town bartering eggs for a little flour to get us through the winter, came running up the path with the letter from Papa, and no thought for her dignity. As she held the letter her hands were trembling so with excitement we could scarcely read Papa's words:

Dear children,

At last we have hope. You will have heard by now how our brave Captain Perry put an end to the British navy on the Great Lakes. The British forces, without the backing of their ships, have deserted the fort at Detroit and have hastened back to Canada, their tails between their legs. We followed closely after them and gained a victory over the British army.

It was my hope that we would turn our forces toward the freeing of Michilimackinac but our commander has decided it is too late in the year for such an undertaking. You will understand how great is my disappointment at having once again to wait out another winter before seeing my beloved children.

We can only rejoice in the victories our forces have achieved and look ahead to the spring and what must surely be our long wished for reunion.

My thoughts are with you every hour of the

day. I know that you are doing your best with the farm. Give my fondest regards to our friends and pray that our long separation will soon be over.

Your loving Papa

You can imagine our joy at hearing from Papa. We hurried to tell everyone the good news. I must confess I took much satisfaction in letting the Wests and the MacNeils know that not only was Papa safe, but that the British army had met with defeat. The Wests and MacNeils had chosen the wrong side after all. If they felt this defeat, they said nothing, but only rejoiced with us. Because of their kindness I felt small at my wishing to lord it over them.

Though the Sinclairs celebrated the American victories as well as Papa's safety, I could see that they were worried about Gavin. Papa's news must mean that those Indians fighting for the British had suffered a defeat.

Mr. Sinclair also had a word of warning. "With the defeat of the British navy all supplies to the fort must be cut off. In the past food came to the fort from the British supply bases on Lake Erie. Now no food will come. Once again the winter will be a hard one."

CHAPTER

HOW MANY TIMES in that hard winter did we read over Papa's letter seeking comfort in Papa's promise of a reunion in spring? The spring of 1814 came and the summer as well. Still there was no sign of the American forces coming to free the island from the British.

With the British navy no longer ruling the lakes, traders began to stop at Michilimackinac on their way west. Nearly every day Jacques would leave some task to run down to the lake to greet their canoes. He would return home with stories of the abundance of pelts to be had beyond the great Mississippi River. "The whole countryside is so full of beavers you can nearly walk about on their backs. In Europe the skins of beavers are so in demand for hats that one trip beyond the Mississippi would make me a rich man."

I knew Jacques was teasing us. Still his restlessness worried me. Besides, all the time he spent listening to the stories of the traders left his work for me to do. No sooner had I brought Belle in from her pasture and milked her than it was time to tend to the hogs. After that the chickens must be fed and watered and their eggs collected. When Jacques neglected to scythe the hay, I scolded him. "What will Belle eat if the hay is left to dry out in the field until it crumbles? And how will the grasses grow up again it they aren't cut back? Papa said we were all to do our tasks. I have to do mine and yours as well."

Jacques answered sullenly, "I won't be tied to a farm all of my life. Why should I spend my time cleaning up after a cow and a bunch of pigs? If Papa thought the farm was so important, why didn't he stay here and take care of it? He went away as soon as he had a chance."

I was horrified. "You should be ashamed of yourself! Papa is risking his life to fight for our country. All you have to do is hoe a little corn and cut some hay. Besides, we promised Papa that we would take care of the farm."

After that Jacques finished his work before he went off to talk with the traders, but he no longer came home to tell us their stories. That was truly frightening, for silence means secrets.

While I worried about what kind of secrets Jacques might have from us, I rejoiced to see Angelique was much more light-hearted. Ever since we had received our letter from Papa she was like a bird who knows one day the door to its cage will fly open. Her prettiness came back. She took more time with her hair and in June's long light nights she cut out and sewed a dress from the New Year's calico, trimming it with a bit of Mama's lace.

Angelique's good spirits were not all because of Papa's letter. A new regiment had been sent to increase the number of soldiers at the fort for the Americans were expected to attack at any time. The new regiment was the Newfoundlanders, a jolly group.

No sooner had they come than they began to organize parties at the fort. It was for the parties that Angelique made her new dress. Elizabeth and Emma were often at our house. While Emma trailed after Jacques expressing admiration for the way he slopped the hogs or shoveled the manure, Elizabeth and Angelique whispered and giggled over this soldier or that. The name of a Lieutenant Daniel Cunningham came often to their lips. According to them he was not only handsome but amiable. As if that were not enough, Lieutenant Cunningham had come from London, England, to join the Newfoundlanders. Angelique and Elizabeth believed there could be no greater advantage than to be a resident of that great city across the sea.

One summer afternoon Lieutenant Cunningham came to our house. He explained that he wished to return a book of poetry that Angelique had lent to him. It was clear to me that the loan was an excuse for the lieutenant and Angelique to see one another. When he left Jacques laughed at the lieutenant for reading poetry. I thought there was much in favor of a soldier who was not ashamed to open a book of poems. Lieutenant Cunningham was indeed pleasing to look at, but Jacques teased Angelique. "His curls are like a girl's," he told her, "and his brown eyes when he looks at you are just like Belle's."

Angelique only said, "Say what you wish, Lieutenant Cunningham is *un homme comme il faut*." If you speak French to people who don't understand you, you can always have the last word.

I was not so angry at the British soldiers as I had been, for the British were losing the war. It is easier to be kind to your enemy when he is losing. Still, I was not happy to have a British soldier in our home. I was even less pleased when a few days after his visit Angelique said that she had asked him to Sunday dinner with us. "Mary, be a dear and take this note from me to the fort so Lieutenant Cunningham may know that we expect him at two o'clock on Sunday."

I grumbled to myself on the way to the fort and took my time in delivering the note. As I dawdled near the Indian camp I overheard the new commander of the fort, Colonel Robert McDouall, giving a speech to the Indian chiefs. It was June 5, which the British celebrate as their king's birthday no matter when their king was born. That way the holiday is likely to be a pleasant day.

For many weeks there had been rumors that an American force was on its way to land on Michilimackinac to win back the island. Colonel

McDouall was thanking the Indians for their loyalty to the British. He said the Americans wanted to take away all of the Indians' land and destroy them. "You possess the warlike spirit of your fathers," he told them. "You can only avoid this horrible fate by joining hand in hand with my warriors in first driving the Big Knives from this island."

I was furious to hear the Americans called "Big Knives" and indignant that lies should be told about them. I was determined to keep Angelique from being seriously engaged with a British soldier. Angrily I tore up her note inviting Lieutenant Cunningham to come at two o'clock. I then marched to the fort, where I asked the sentry to send for Lieutenant Cunningham. By now the sentry knew me well from my daily trips with milk and eggs.

"Well, miss, the lieutenant has something better to do than come to the gate and chat with you. If you have a message you can give it to me and I'll pass it on to Lieutenant Cunningham."

"It's very important you get it right," I said.

"Make it short and simple and you'll have no worry on that score," he promised.

"You must tell Lieutenant Cunningham that he is expected at our house for dinner Sunday at one o'clock sharp." I repeated the "one o'clock sharp" and then ran off.

On Sunday Angelique hurried home after church. As I knew she would, she put her curls up in rags and pulled on her oldest dress with the elbows poked out and her apron with the torn pockets to do the cooking. It was a warm day but a fire had to be lighted in the fireplace to cook the partridge Jacques had shot for our lunch. The heat from the fire made Angelique perspire, and when she wiped her face, the soot from her hand made long smudges on her face. So hot did it grow in the room that as she fussed over the gooseberry trifle she kicked off her shoes and pulled off her stockings.

As she flew around the house barefooted she ordered Jacques and me about. Jacques was to round up the hens from the walkway and shut them into the henhouse. "In London," she said, "there can be no chickens running about the fine houses."

I was sent to gather a bouquet of flowers from the garden for the dinner table. When at last everything was in order, Angelique started up to the loft to wash and change. It was not quite one o'clock. "Wait," I said. "I can't manage the flowers. They're all a tangle."

Angelique shook her head at my efforts. "Let me rearrange them. I have another hour before Lieutenant Cunningham comes." As she was hastily pushing the flowers about there was a knock on the door. Because of the heat in the room, we had left the door half open and now Lieutenant Cunningham walked into the room.

Angelique was too surprised to make a dash for the ladder to the loft. There was a horrified look on her face. All she could say was, "But you weren't supposed to be here until two. My note expressly said two."

"Oh, it's you, Angelique," Lieutenant Cunningham said. "I didn't recognize you at first. I apologize if I have come at the wrong time, but the sentry said that Mary expressly told him one o'clock." They both looked at me: The lieutenant with a puzzled look and my sister with a look that shriveled me. I didn't care. I was sure that having seen Angelique all untidy and sooty with her hair in rags, the lieutenant would go away and never return.

I will give Angelique credit. She stretched her neck up as far as it could go and said, "If you will pardon me, Lieutenant Cunningham, I will excuse myself for a moment. My dear sister will doubtless be pleased to entertain you. I am certain there are many little embarrassing stories about me she can summon forth, given so good an opportunity." With that she turned her back and ascended the ladder to the loft, exposing the soiled bottoms of her bare feet.

Lieutenant Cunningham turned to me. "What does she mean?" Luckily Jacques appeared at that moment to interrupt us with a tale of a hawk that had nearly snatched one of our new chicks.

The only thing that saved me from my sister's wrath after the lieutenant left that evening was the parting smile he gave Angelique as he said, "If other young ladies could look half so pretty as you do with rag curlers in your hair and bare feet, it would surely start a fashion."

CHAPTER

13

*E*ARLY IN JULY we learned the Americans had defeated the British at Prairie du Chien on the Mississippi. Alarmed, Colonel McDouall was sure the Americans were on their way to retake Michilimackinac. Soon afterward Angelique heard from Lieutenant Cunningham that a fleet of American ships had sailed into Lake Huron and was even now heading toward our island. Suddenly the fort was on alert and there were no more parties or visits from the Lieutenant. I worried that Papa would be on board the ship with the troops. As much as I longed to see him, if there was to be fighting, something might happen to him.

Early in July the British placed cannons on the high ground above the fort. Each day the men drilled and practiced shooting their cannons. At the same time Indians friendly to the British were summoned to the island. It was reported that Gavin and his people were among them.

Jacques had seen the Sinclairs standing at a distance from the Indian camp hoping for a glimpse of Gavin. They did not seek him out, though, for they would not go among Indians pledged to fight on the side of the British. The Indians were often in the fort drilling with the soldiers.

In anticipation of the battle the townspeople were storing food. I would not sell our food to the fort any longer, knowing it could only add strength to the British. "Our cow is about to have a calf," I lied to the quartermaster, "and our chickens were carried away by an eagle."

The quartermaster gave me a suspicious look. "Well, I would as soon believe you if you had told me the cow was carried away by an eagle and your chickens were having a calf." I am not a good liar.

Jacques could think of nothing but of joining in the battle against the British. Angelique was worried for Papa. Though she said nothing, I knew she worried for her lieutenant as well.

In the middle of July we heard that the Americans had burned the British fort on nearby St. Joseph Island. The American forces were under the command of a colonel from Kentucky. "He is only twenty-two," Jacques said, envy in his voice. "That means he is a mere five years older than I am." Angelique and I watched with alarm as Jacques left his farm chores to patch his canoe. We worried even more when he spent hours at the Indian camp trying to learn what he could about the battle with the Americans that was sure to come.

It was a Saturday morning when Jacques made a great fuss about gathering together his fishing supplies. "Pere Mercier and I are going out in the canoe. You need not keep dinner for me," he said. "In this hot weather the whitefish are in deep water. I may not be back until late." He gave both of us a long look, as though our faces were a lesson he had been set to memorize. It was only after he was gone for some time that we noticed Papa's Brown Bess musket was not in its place on the wall.

I went at once to St. Anne's, where I found Pere Mercier trimming his rosebushes. "You aren't fishing with Jacques?" I asked.

"As you see." He smiled at me. "On a hot summer afternoon like this even I could not believe the fish would be biting."

I told him we feared that Jacques had gone to join the American forces.

He shook his head. "I'm afraid there is little we can do, Mary. Your brother has done a foolish thing, but he is a young man now and must make up his own mind. This island rightly belongs to the Americans. I think if I were not a priest and an old man, I would have gone with him."

The next days were hard. Pere Mercier warned us to tell no one what Jacques had done for fear the news would reach the fort. If he were to be captured, Jacques might be accused of treason. We took a long time over our prayers each night. When friends asked for Jacques we said he was away hunting on the mainland.

Early in the morning of July 26, word flew around the island that the American fleet had been sighted. As the ships were recognized people called out their names: the *Lawrence*, the

Niagara, the *Tigress*, the *Caledonia*, and the *Scorpion*. Their very names cheered us. No sooner had we sighted the ships than a terrible storm began to blow over the island. Trees were shaken by the winds. Their branches bowed down to the ground in the terrible gusts. Black clouds crushed the light from the sky. Lightning and thunder tortured us all the day and into the night. The waves surged and slapped the shore. Whitecaps tossed the ships. One by one they pulled away from the island. This brought great relief to the fort and to those on the island who were on the side of the British.

Angelique and I huddled together in our cabin, trying to comfort one another. "If there is a battle, Jacques and Lieutenant Cunningham will both be killed," Angelique sobbed. "Why cannot countries be civil to one another? Why must men be always shooting at one another? Women don't shoot at each other."

"I would shoot at the British if I had Papa's musket," I said.

"And I suppose you would kill Lieutenant Cunningham?"

I was silent, for I did not think I could kill anyone who looked at me with eyes like Belle's.

I knew I could not shoot at Gavin, whose beads I wore hidden under my dress.

On Sunday Pere Mercier preached the Sermon on the Mount. "Blessed are the peacemakers, for they shall be called the children of God," he recited. There were many British soldiers and many British citizens in the church, so he could not say as much as he wished. Still, when he came to "whosoever is angry with his brother without a cause shall be in danger of the judgment," he looked hard at the British soldiers. Lieutenant Cunningham had the decency to blush.

The next morning the whole island awakened to the pounding of cannons. Small boats filled with American troops were reported to be making for the northwest shore. It was said there were as many as four hundred Americans. Colonel McDouall with a hundred and fifty soldiers and twice that number of Indians marched from the fort toward the landing site to meet the American attack.

The townspeople were urged to take refuge in the fort and many did. Angelique and I stayed in our cabin. We did not want to leave the animals lest they be stolen. Besides, we did not believe we had anything to fear from the Americans.

We learned the American forces and the British forces were facing one another on a large field only a few miles from our farm. Soon we began to hear the firing of muskets. Each shot felt as though it were piercing my own heart. It was the same for Angelique, who clamped a pillow over her ears. Soon the cannons sounded. On and on the shooting went until I could stand it no more.

"Where are you going?" Angelique asked.

"To see if Belle is all right. Loud noises frighten her. I don't want her jumping the fence." Instead I hurried past Belle and toward the noise of the battle.

The hot sun beat down on me. With every step the grasshoppers in my path flew up against me like tiny green bullets. As I drew near, out of breath and sweating, the sounds of the cannons and muskets were deafening. Clouds of dust filled the air. I heard men's cries like the howls of wild beasts. Concealed by the trunk of a large pine tree, I peered out at the field of battle. There before me I saw hundreds of men. The Americans were lined up into two rows. The British soldiers were strung out in a single row. In the middle of their ranks were two cannons pointed at the American soldiers. I saw there were more Americans than British and for a moment I was hopeful, but suddenly with loud cries, hundreds of Indians appeared on either side of the battlefield and began to advance against the Americans.

As I watched, an American soldier fell to the ground, his blue jacket turning crimson with blood. An American officer with his sword unsheathed ran at a British soldier who was loading his musket. I waited not a moment longer. I tucked up my skirts and ran as fast as I could until I reached our cabin, where I flung my arms around Angelique and burst into sobs. "They will all kill one another! We will never see Papa or Jacques or Gavin or Lieutenant Cunningham alive again!"

"What do you mean?" Angelique gasped. "Where have you been? What have you heard?"

"It is what I saw. I never thought it to be like that." It was true. I knew that rows of soldiers shot at one another, but my imagination had never gone so far as to picture their being hurt. I would never forget the bloody jacket of the stricken soldier.

All day we prayed for the cannons to be

silent, yet we were fearful of what we would find when they quieted. At last the silence came. We waited for some word, not wanting to leave the cabin lest a message should come. Like us, the Sinclairs had stayed on their farm and knew as little as we did. Pere Mercier was on the battlefield with the wounded and dead. Dr. West tended the wounded, and Mrs. West with Elizabeth and Emma had gone to the safety of the fort. It was the blacksmith, Mr. MacNeil, who came to tell us that the fighting was over. The defeated American troops had returned to their ships and were sailing away.

"I do not believe your papa was there, but someone said they thought they saw Jacques," said Mr. MacNeil. "How can that be? Did you know he had gone to fight with the Americans?"

Hastily Angelique said, "They must have mistaken another soldier for Jacques. He left this morning for a hunting trip to St. Ignace." With a trembling voice she asked, "What of the British soldiers? Have any been killed?"

"At this moment I know of none," he said. "It is the Americans who suffered the greatest loss. Their commander and twelve privates were killed. The number of their wounded is much greater."

Moments after Mr. MacNeil had left us, the door to the cabin was flung open and Jacques burst inside. He was covered with dirt. His clothes were torn and there was blood on his face. Angelique and I would have screamed but for Jacques' warning. "Hush! Would you bring Mr. MacNeil back?"

"Jacques," I said, "I saw the battlefield. It was terrible."

Jacques looked startled. "You had no business coming there. Men were shooting in all directions. You might have been hit."

I had never thought of that and my knees went weak. "But you were there. It was more dangerous for you."

"I went aboard their ships to see if Papa was with them. One of the soldiers who knew him said he was still in Detroit at Fort Wayne. I begged the Americans to let me fight with them. They said I was only a boy. They told me since I was not a member of the army I could not go into battle with them. But an old sergeant saw how disappointed I was. He told me as I had a musket and as they needed all the help they could get, once the fighting started no one would stop me.

"It was all I could do not to run away from

the battle. The cannons were trained on us and the Indians were making so much noise. Suddenly there was Gavin in front of me." At Gavin's name I clenched my hands until my nails bit into my palms.

Jacques was too excited to notice my distress and went on with his story. "We had both raised our muskets and were prepared to fire when we recognized one another. We held our fire. It was then I realized I was not meant for a soldier. Soon after, retreat was sounded and the Americans began to withdraw. I knew the woods well enough to slip away."

As soon as I could catch my breath, I asked, "And Gavin?"

Jacques shook his head. "I cannot say."

We soon found that Jacques had only a bad scratch, which Angelique quickly dressed with a salve of sweet elder bark and wrapped with flannel. "Jacques, Mr. MacNeil says that you were recognized," I told him.

"It will make no difference. I am going away. Winter will be coming on and the Americans will not be back until next spring. I will not stay here with the British."

"But Jacques, where will you go?" Angelique asked.

"I'll leave with the first trader who will take me. The Gauthiers should be here soon. They were sighted by some Indians no more than a few days from here."

I couldn't believe that Jacques would leave us. "What about our farm?"

"In spite of what happened today, everyone says the war is sure to be over by next summer. Then Papa will be back. There won't be much to do this winter. It would be best to sell the pigs and Belle for meat. The rest you can manage."

"Kill Belle! And cut her up to eat! Jacques! What are you saying?"

"Well, at least sell the pigs. If I stay here I will certainly be reported to the British and they will arrest me. What good would I be to you then?"

*I*N THE CONFUSION that followed the battle we were left to ourselves. Angelique slipped out the next afternoon to inquire at the fort. She was greatly relieved to learn Lieutenant Cunningham had suffered no more than a badly wrenched knee. It would keep him confined to quarters but would present no lasting problem.

Everyone on the island believed that the American forces would come again in the spring, this time in larger numbers so that they were sure to be successful. Yet it was hard to keep up our hopes. It had been over two years since Papa had left us. The dress I had worn on the day I said farewell to him was now too small for me. The sleeves ended well above my wrists, and the hem an immodest three inches above my ankles. Our third winter was coming on. This time we would not have Jacques to help us. There was sure to be a shortage of food on the island, for we had learned that before sailing back to Detroit, the Americans had scuttled the British destroyer *Nancy*, which was on its way to supply the fort. There was no other British ship to bring the island much-needed supplies. I would not be sorry to see the British want for food but I was not eager to join them in their hunger.

Only days after the battle Jacques began his preparations to leave. As yet no one had reported his part in the battle to the fort. Still he was careful to stay out of sight. He brought firewood from the woods to last us the winter. He gathered maple leaves to use as bedding for the henhouse. The only time he left the farm was to take Belle for her yearly visit with Jupiter. He knew that he could trust M. André.

One night when the moon was high, Jacques shot a deer so that we would have meat to salt away for the winter. He made part of his kill into jerky to take with him on his journey. After boiling strips of the lean venison he salted them and hung them in the sun until they shriveled and dried.

Angelique and I were put to work to knit him warm gloves and a cap. Jacques would be traveling in cold country and living in rough camps rather than warm cabins.

Late in September, just as the tamarack trees turned gold and the gulls were getting restless, M. and Mme. Gauthier's canoe reached our island. With the defeat of the British ships the lakes were once again open to the fur trade. Jacques waited until night fell and then made his way down to the Gauthiers. When he returned he was elated.

"They will take me with them," he told us. "They need help in carrying the canoe on the portages."

"Where will you go?" I asked, dreading the answer.

"We will cross Lake Michigan. From there we take the Fox River to the Mississippi. Our winter camp will be among the Sioux at the mouth of the Rock River." He could not keep the excitement from his voice.

"But Jacques," I said, "there has been fighting there between the Americans and the British."

"With all the empty miles of woods and prairie we will have no trouble knowing how to stay away from the fighting."

The next morning we saw in the distance the red coat of a British soldier coming toward our cabin. Jacques hastily crawled out the back window. Angelique, hoping it was Lieutenant Cunningham, flung open the door. She was disappointed to find the soldier was a sergeant who had been sent to bring Jacques to the fort. The sergeant was old for a soldier, a little stooped and with white hair. He was not unfriendly but he was firm in his intention. "I beg your pardon, ma'am," he said to Angelique. "I understand you have a brother, Jacques O'Shea. Up at the fort they would like to question him." All the while he spoke, his eyes were searching our cabin for evidence of what he sought.

"Why would they want to question my brother?" I asked. I made my voice as innocent as I could.

"Well, miss, I wouldn't know that. I was just told to bring him along."

"He left early this morning to go fishing," Angelique said.

The sergeant looked at the rack on the wall, which held Jacques' fishing things. "It looks as if your brother has gone off without his poles. Odd. Once I give my report up at the fort, I can promise you I will be back and I won't come alone. If your brother doesn't turn himself in, we will have to take him in chains. We can have no traitors on this island, even young and foolish ones. Things will go much easier for him if he gives himself up. Meanwhile, for my trouble, I'll just help myself to one of your chickens."

I glared at him. "Then you may give yourself up at the fort as well. Tell them that you are a thief who steals from helpless women. See if they don't put *you* in chains."

His face reddened as he stared down at me. "Not so helpless," he laughed. We watched him walk away. He lingered for a moment by the henhouse but he took no chicken with him.

The moment he was out of sight Jacques climbed down from the maple tree behind the house. Hastily he gathered his clothes and supplies together. "But you can't go," I protested. "I still have two fingers to knit on your gloves." I was looking for any excuse to keep him there. First Papa had left us and now Jacques was deserting us.

Angelique said, "How will we manage by ourselves?"

"What good would I do you if I were imprisoned in the guardhouse at the fort? Prisoners can be shot for treason."

We were so frightened by those terrible words we made no further protest. Angelique helped him with his packing while I stood guard by the window looking out for more British soldiers. As soon as it was dark, Jacques slung his knapsack over his shoulder. Taking Papa's musket, he turned to say good-bye to us. We both clung to him. All three of us were crying. I could not remember ever seeing Jacques cry, though Angelique had told me once that when Mama died, Jacques would not stop crying.

We stood at the cabin door watching our brother disappear into the dark woods. I had never felt so alone. Earlier in the week a loon had settled in a nearby pond to molt. That night we heard the loon's wild cry. There is no more lonesome cry in the world. I believe the loon was grieving with us.

15

$\mathcal{A}$T FIRST WE WERE SURE the war would be over in the spring and we had only to get through one more winter. But soon the frightening news spread over the island that the British troops had marched into our capital city of Washington. There they entered the White House and finished the dinner President Madison and his wife, Dolly, had been forced to leave behind as they fled the city. The British then proceeded to burn down much of Washington. "After such news surely there can be no more meetings between you and Lieutenant Cunningham," I said to Angelique.

She was stubborn. "Lieutenant Cunningham would not burn a building down for anything."

We had no time for quarrels. Without Jacques we labored from sunup to sundown at work we were not used to. To split wood I had to wield a heavy axe. When the first snow fell Angelique was outside with the snow shovel. It was a great relief when the Sinclairs kindly offered to take the pigs so we would not have to sell them. Mr. Sinclair promised, "We will only keep them until your papa comes home. Then you shall have them back." In return for their kindness we made them agree to accept one of the pigs for their own.

They offered to care for Belle also. "Let them have her," Angelique pleaded. "That way we won't have to be bothered with milking and making butter."

"I couldn't let them take Belle." The only time of day when I could safely cry, without making Angelique sad as well, was when I was in the shed milking Belle. I would rest my head against her warm flank and cry as much as I liked. I knew from the melancholy look in Belle's large brown eyes that she understood how I felt. Besides, the Sinclairs would not rub her under the chin every day, which was her favorite treat.

"You have to lug gallons of water to Belle three times a day and you have to milk her twice a day. And Mary, think what it will be like to have to clean her shed each night."

"I won't give up Belle. You take care of the hens and I'll take care of Belle." Up until the snows came I could roll the wheelbarrow from the shed and pitch the manure over the fields. Once the snow covered the ground there was nothing to do but make a huge manure pile behind the shed as Jacques had always done. When I came home each afternoon from my task, Angelique was waiting for me with a tub of hot water and a bar of soap.

Only days before the lake froze over, a boat arrived with mail. At last we had a letter from Papa.

My dear children,

I have only time for a hasty note. Our defeat on Michilimackinac was a great disappointment.

Had it only been otherwise I might now be with my beloved family. Last winter our forces here in Detroit were greatly weakened by an epidemic of cholera. Hundreds of our soldiers died, so many that there were not enough caskets in which to bury them. I thank God that I was spared, but it was necessary for me to remain here, for our forces protecting Fort Wayne are few in number.

You must get through one more winter. I am sure that with the help of Jacques, who can do a man's work, you will manage. When the war comes to an end you can be sure I will take the first means of reaching the island and my children, whom I think of and pray for each hour of the day.

Your loving Papa

We read the letter so many times it began to give way at the folds. What would Papa say if he knew Jacques had left us? I resolved that when Papa returned, the farm should be just as he wished.

Winter came on in a rush. The snow fell day after day so that it seemed there would be no more room for it. Each morning Angelique and I had to dig a path from our cabin to Belle's shed and the henhouse. The snow hung down in scallops from our roof. It piled up from the ground.

One morning we awoke to find that the snow from the roof and the snow from the ground had met and we could no longer see out of our windows. "We shall drown in the snow," Angelique groaned. "The cabin will be buried and we will not be found until spring."

We took up our shovels, and putting on all the clothes we had, we pushed open the door and went outside into the winter morning. Angelique could not leave the chickens without food and water. I had to milk and feed and water Belle, who was restless from her long imprisonment in the shed. She stamped her hooves and swished her tail so much I tied it up to keep it from tipping the milk pail.

Buildings made of stone are not very warm. With nothing to heat it but Belle's warmth, it was so cold in the shed that I had to break a layer of ice on Belle's water bowl. Angelique carried the eggs from the henhouse to the cabin inside her bodice so they would not freeze.

I made a frightening discovery that morning. Belle's hay was giving out. In his hurry with the harvest Jacques had left some of the hay uncut. Soon Belle would run out of food. No one on the island had hay to spare. The fort had bought or confiscated as much hay as they could find. It was only through Lieutenant Cunningham's efforts that our own small supply had not been taken.

I was horrified to hear Angelique say, "It would be better to kill Belle while she is fat than wait until she starves to death."

Desperate, I recalled something. "When Belle was out in the pasture I saw her chewing on twigs and branches like a deer," I told Angelique. "There are no leaves now but there are buds on the trees."

I set out into the woods on snowshoes carrying the saw and a basket. Once I was a little way from the farm, the world became perfectly still and white and so bright I became dizzy. The snowflakes fell on my eyelashes so that my lids became heavy and I could hardly see. My tracks on the path disappeared. I thought of Jacques. It was as though he were right there with me. He would be out in the winter snows, going from Indian camp to Indian camp for furs. He would travel long distances on solitary rivers edged with ice. At the end of his long journeys he would return to no warm cabin. I knew our winter was not so hard as his.

Belle ate the tree loppings I cut for her each

day. Without the hay to feed on she gave very little milk, but the weather was so bad we were not able to get down to the village to sell what little she gave. Angelique and I ate eggs and cabbage and kale and carrots. We were nearly out of flour so bread was a Sunday treat. A little venison remained from Jacques' deer and the Wests had given us maple syrup, which we sometimes had on our porridge.

On the first day the weather cleared we went down into the village to trade eggs for flour, only to find there was no flour to be had. The winter was as hard for everyone as it was for us. It was harder for those who had no farm produce to fall back on as we did.

When next we went into the village we brought a basket of turnips and cabbage and carrots to leave with Pere Mercier to give out to those who were in need. "We suffer here in the village," he said, "but I hear it is even worse at the fort. There were no boats to supply them this fall and there is nothing in the village to buy. The soldiers have had to kill their horses for something to eat." I thought of the handsome horse the commander rode and wondered how he could make a dinner of it.

That afternoon we had a visit from Lieutenant

Cunningham. He came through the door shaking the snow from his coat and stamping his boots. It was the first time Angelique had seen him since the battle. He took her hand and held it for a long while. And she let him. Urging him to warm himself at the fire, she said, "Let me make you some blackberry tea. There are corn cakes left from our dinner and honey."

The lieutenant eagerly sat down to feast on the food Angelique put before him. He appeared so hungry I said nothing about his eating the last of our honey. Angelique sat across from him looking as though there was no finer sight in the world than that of a man licking honey from his fingers. If it had been me, she would have scolded me for my bad manners.

He must have guessed what I was thinking for he said, "I apologize for my behavior. You will forgive me when you learn there is little to eat at the fort."

I couldn't help asking, "Is it true you are eating up all your horses?"

"The horses were gone long ago. It is for that reason that I am here. There are unscrupulous men on the island who come by night to steal the animals from the farms. They then sell them to the quartermaster at the fort for high prices. We are so desperate for food no questions are asked as to how the animals are come by. Today in the fort I overheard two of these scheming men ask how much a cow would bring. Knowing you have one I wanted to warn you. I would offer to protect your animal myself but we are not allowed out of the fort at night. I am sure Colonel McDouall would never stand for such behavior, but no one has the courage to tell him of the thefts, nor the proof to set before him."

I was horrified. "How could they get Belle to the fort?"

"I'm afraid they would shoot her and butcher her. Knapsacks on the backs of two strong men would carry a good deal of meat. Now I must get back." We thanked him and Angelique urged him to come again for a meal.

"What can we do?" Angelique asked after he left. "Perhaps we could ask Mr. Sinclair's help."

"He must guard his own animals. We'll have to think of something else." I hurried out to the shed to reassure myself that Belle was all right. As I rubbed her under the chin an idea came to me. The door into the stone shed was made of a thick slab of wood. It was fastened by sliding a heavy bar across the door. I put Belle's halter on and led her outside. At first she would not walk through the snow, but with gentle urging she stepped along and seemed almost frisky at being out of doors. Her warm breath made little clouds of fog and every so often she would stop to nip playfully at a snow bank. At last we were at the door of the cabin. I opened it and as I began to pull her inside Angelique screamed.

"Mary! What are you thinking of? We cannot have a cow in the house! You must be out of your mind." She picked up a broom and began to shoo Belle away.

"Put down the broom. It is only for one night. We can't let those evil men murder her. I'd rather they shot me." Quickly I told Angelique my plan.

At first she refused to go along with it. "If they catch us they will murder us."

I pleaded and pleaded, all the while drawing Belle farther into the cabin until I could close the door behind her. The moment I let her loose she began to chew a bunch of dried herbs that hung from one of the cabin beams.

"Stop it, Belle." Angelique swung the broom. "That's my rosemary." She looked about the cabin for a place to put Belle, but there was no place suitable for a very large cow. Belle, however, looked quite happy in her new home, which was much warmer than her stone shed.

We dragged her to a corner of the cabin and tied her securely. Hastily we carried away everything within her reach. When we were done Angelique sank down on a chair.

"If you don't want to do it," I said, "I'll do it myself."

"Mary, what have we come to? A cow in the house and you wanting to risk your life? I would never forgive myself if something happened to you."

In spite of her protests, when the time came, Angelique was ready. I think she was willing to go along with my plan just to be sure that Belle would not be spending more nights in our cabin. As the last bit of daylight disappeared we hurried into the henhouse. By opening the door a crack we could easily see the cow shed, which was just across the path.

The hens were used to Angelique's daily visits. After some fluttering and squawking they returned to their roosts and settled down again for the night. As we huddled together to keep warm we could not tell whether our shivering was from cold or fright. We didn't dare whisper for fear of being heard so we had to pass the time in silence.

I had no idea of how long we had been there when we heard muffled voices. Peering out of the crack in the door we saw two men with a lantern approaching the cow shed. We clutched one another and the movement stirred up one of the hens, who squawked. The men stopped in their tracks and looked toward the henhouse. When after a minute the men heard nothing more, they must have decided it was their approach that had disturbed the hen.

One of the men held up the lantern while the other pulled the bar from its slot and opened the door. Together they slipped into the shed. As Angelique and I dashed toward the shed I could hear one of the men exclaim, "The cow is gone!" Quickly I slid the bar back into its slot, sealing the door. We held our breath. For a moment there was silence. Then there were sounds of pushing and heaving against the door. Then silence again. More heaving and striking of the door with heavy boots. There were cries of, "Let us out! We're gentle folk that don't mean harm to a living soul! We wouldn't touch a hair on your head."

A moment later we heard terrible shouts.

"Let us out or we'll crush every bone in your body! We'll boil you in oil! We'll tear you apart!"

When we were sure that there was no way the two men could break through the stone shed or the heavy wooden door, Angelique and I returned to the house, where Belle had made herself too much at home.

"It will be very cold out there," Angelique said.

"It cannot be too cold for those evil men," I replied. "Anyhow it will only be until morning."

We were too agitated to sleep so we barred our door and waited for daylight. When it came I wrapped myself up, and putting on Angelique's boots, which were in better condition than mine, I set out for the fort.

The sentry, a soldier I did not recall seeing before, looked both cold and sleepy. "I wish to see Colonel McDouall," I said in my haughtiest manner.

"Our commander has better things to do than come running out to see you." In a brusque voice he added, "Get along now."

"Please tell the commander I have locked up two criminals who have been doing business with his fort."

At this the sentry's eyebrows flew up and his mouth hung open. "What's that?"

I repeated my message, pleased at his reaction. He gave me a long unbelieving look but finally he called to a soldier inside the fort and repeated my request. This soldier looked equally skeptical but went off toward the commander's quarters. As we waited, the sentry kept his eye on me as if I were a snake that might strike at him the moment he turned his back.

My courage began to fail me. What if the commander didn't believe me? And even if he did, he might not care. He might even be angry that the fort would not have a cow to eat.

Colonel McDouall was a smallish man for a commander. His uniform was none too neat, his jacket was unbuttoned and his hat sat on one side of his head. His manner was stern. "Speak up, miss. What do you want?" he asked.

"There are two men who have been stealing farm animals and selling them to your quartermaster. Last night they came to steal our cow but we locked them in the cow shed. They are still there."

"What! You accuse my quartermaster of buying stolen property! I don't believe a word of it." He straightened his hat and began to button his jacket.

"Then you had better come and see for yourself," I said.

"Very well. I shall do just that." He turned to a captain who stood beside him. "Captain Thompson, you will accompany me. All right, young lady, lead on. But if this is some sort of mischief, I'll have you over my knee."

I led the way and the commander and the captain followed along, the commander grumbling at every turn. "What thanks is this," he said, "after years of service to my country, to be posted in this godforsaken place where instead of marshaling great battles I must attend to the stealing of cows."

When we reached the cabin Angelique came running out to meet us. The men were still beating on the door and crying out. The commander now looked less skeptical. "Is the cow in there with them?" he asked.

"No, sir," I said. "It is in the house."

"The house! Is that customary?"

Angelique was mortified. "No, indeed, sir. It was only for last night."

At the sound of the commander's voice the men had become quiet. The captain was about to unbolt the door when I stopped him. I called out to the two prisoners, "If you want to get out you must answer my question."

There was silence for a moment and then through chattering teeth a voice said, "Ask your question but be quick about it. We are freezing to death."

"You must tell the truth or we won't open the door. You can just stay there. Who were you going to sell the cow to?" I demanded.

"Brown, the quartermaster, of course. Who else?"

At this the commander himself marched up to the door and pushed back the bolt. As the men rushed out they found the captain and the commander both with muskets at the ready. In a stern voice the commander asked if we had a length of rope handy. At first we thought the men were to be hanged before our eyes but the rope was only wanted to truss them. Angelique fetched it from the cabin.

"I am greatly indebted to you young ladies," the commander said. "You have accomplished what my whole regiment was evidently unable to manage. I myself will handle the quartermaster. Now, before we leave I would just like a peek at the cow."

"Oh, sir," Angelique protested. "It is not tidy in the cabin just now."

"Yes, yes. I can understand how that could be. Well, if it is not convenient at the moment, perhaps you will let me call another time."

We both eagerly assured him that he would be most welcome. They were scarcely out of sight when Angelique hurried into the cabin to get Belle out of the house. Belle did not want to leave the warmth of the fireside and it took the two of us all of a half hour of pushing and pulling to return Belle to her shed.

That afternoon a soldier arrived from the fort. "The commander sends his compliments, ladies," he said. He handed us a good-sized packet, saluted, and left us. Eagerly we untied the string. Inside was a large packet of sugar. And not just ordinary sugar but pure white sugar such as I had never seen and Angelique only just recollected from living in Detroit. That night we had a pinch of sugar on everything, even the turnips.

CHAPTER

16

*C*LOSED OFF BY THE ICE all around us we
had no way of knowing, but something wondrous had happened that winter. Far away in the
country of Belgium, in the town of Ghent, a
treaty was signed by America and England. The
war was over! First the news of peace crossed
the great ocean. Then it made its way to us
across America and over the melting spring
waters of the lakes. There was a great celebration on the island, for we knew that soon

Michilimackinac would be returned to the Americans. Most important of all for Angelique and me, Papa would be coming home.

Those who had taken an oath of allegiance to the British were forgiven. Pere Mercier invited everyone to St. Anne's, where we gave thanks for the end of the war. Even some of the British soldiers came. They were sorry to lose, but I believe many of them were pleased to be leaving our harsh winters and narrow borders. Only Lieutenant Cunningham appeared unhappy. From the way he looked at Angelique with his cow's eyes, I guessed why he was not anxious to leave Michilimackinac. I thought the sooner he left the better.

After the service, the Wests kindly engaged us to dine with them. It was there that I learned the shocking news.

The Wests have a proper house right in town rather than a rough cabin like ours. The rooms are all whitewashed and the sitting room has little flowers and ivy stenciled on the walls. The furniture is dainty and the curtains silk, although their daughter, Elizabeth, once told Angelique the curtains were fashioned from an old dress of Mrs. West's. I believed that possible, for the windows were small and Mrs. West large. The table was nicely set with china so thin you could see your fingers through the cups when you drank. The heavy spoons were marked with a lion, which means they were of real silver.

As we were finishing our pudding Mrs. West said, "We were sure all would be well and the Americans would be victorious."

"Having the British soldiers here cannot have been so bad a thing for everyone," Elizabeth said.

Hearing such a remark made me forget how we were to forgive one another. "How can you say that?" I asked. "Didn't the British soldiers shoot down some of our American soldiers?"

Elizabeth looked slyly at Angelique. "I believe it has been a very good thing for one British soldier and for someone at our table as well."

"Yes, indeed," Dr. West said. "Only this morning Colonel McDouall informed me of the good news. He has given Lieutenant Cunningham his permission. He recalls how Mary and Angelique caught the cow thieves. 'Why then,' Colonel McDouall said, 'should not one of them catch an officer?' "

I was horrified. I could not believe that my sister would actually choose for a husband a man who had waged war against her father and brother. And that everyone should know of it but me, her own flesh and blood! I glared at Angelique, who went all red in the face.

Mrs. West saw our discomfort and quickly changed the subject. "Angelique, you must let me have your mama's recipe for red currant jam. As soon as I can get them I mean to put in a row of currant bushes."

Emma asked, as she always did, if we had heard anything from Jacques. "Surely he will be returning soon. Already the first canoes of the traders are reaching the island."

No further word was said about Lieutenant Cunningham. It was only my good manners that made me bite my tongue and say nothing of what I felt. But I had all I could do to choke down my food.

It was late in the afternoon when the Wests waved us good-bye. The moment we were out of sight of their house, I took hold of Angelique and made her look at me. "What did Dr. West mean when he said Lieutenant Cunningham had received permission? Permission for what?"

Angelique sank down on a tuft of green moss and pulled me down next to her. From where we sat we could see the fort above and the town below, where the smoke from Sunday afternoon's cooking fires drifted over the houses.

She could not look at me but with her eyes upon the ground she said in a low voice, "I meant to tell you before you heard it elsewhere. Lieutenant Cunningham and I are engaged. He asked me for my hand two months ago but I would not agree while we were still at war." Her voice became stubborn. "Now that there is peace, and we are no longer enemies, you can have nothing against him."

It was true that apart from his being British, I could find nothing to complain of in the lieutenant. His warning had saved Belle. He had even promised that as soon as the soldiers received new mounts, he would let me ride his horse. Still, there was something that troubled me. "Angelique, Lieutenant Cunningham will resign from the army and stay here on the island, won't he?" I couldn't believe my sister would leave us.

She put her arm around me and drew me close. "Mary, that is my only sadness. Daniel's family live in London, where they have a business importing cotton from America. His father is not well and expects Daniel to leave the army and return to London to mind the business."

"I will never see you again," I wailed.

"Yes, indeed you will. Daniel says he will travel to America to buy cotton. He promises to take me with him. And Mary, you can come to visit me in London. Surely you would like that."

"Leave the island and go all the way across the ocean! I couldn't." But already I was imagining myself walking through Westminster Abbey or boating on the Thames or even going down to Windsor Palace to pay a visit to King George. I would be very cross with the king for picking a fight with our country. "Angelique, what will Papa think of your marrying Lieutenant Cunningham?"

"I've told Daniel I can't marry him until Papa returns and gives his permission. I believe, though, that Papa will be happy for me, for I love Daniel so, and Daniel is such a good man."

At that I got up and started back to the cabin. I could see Angelique was getting sentimental. I did not think I would ever fall in love, for it made you stupid and foolish beyond anything.

CHAPTER

17

*F*ROM THAT DAY ON Angelique and I met every schooner and trader and Indian canoe that arrived on the island, hoping that it would bring news of Papa or Jacques. All we could learn was that the Americans were fitting out the Second U.S. Regiment of Riflemen under Colonel Anthony Butler. Any day they would set sail to reclaim Michilimackinac. We were sure Papa would be on that ship.

Perhaps the peace brought a blessing with it, for as summer came on everything flourished. Mr. Sinclair brought his horses to help us plow the cornfield. It seemed that no sooner did we bury the kernels of seed corn in the black earth than green shoots pushed up. In the chicken house the hens had been brooding and now twenty chicks pecked their way out of their eggs. Belle was expecting her new calf any day.

The woods were a prodigious bouquet of wildflowers. One Sunday Angelique gathered purple-and-yellow violets to preserve for her wedding cake. She beat up the white of an egg, then dipped the violets into the foam and into some of the white sugar Colonel McDouall had given us. The dried violets looked like crystal flowers.

The fragrance of lilacs hung everywhere over the island. Each yard had a lilac bush. The lilacs had been brought long ago by schooner from the east coast and even as far away as England and France. As soon as someone built a house or started a farm they planted a lilac. If they didn't have a bush of their own they begged a slip from a neighbor to start one. Sometimes the house or the farm was abandoned, but the lilac bushes stubbornly hung on, refusing to give up. For that reason lilacs are my favorite flower.

With the end of the war everything changed. Like the great flocks of geese that suddenly appear from nowhere to fill the spring skies, the French Canadian and the British and American fur traders swarmed over the island on their way north. It was said that John Jacob Astor himself would come to Michilimackinac to set up a fur trading company. The Indians were returning by the hundreds: the Sauk, the Menomonee, the Chippewa, the Winnebagoe, and the Ottawa. I did not see how any place on earth could be more exciting than our island.

One evening Angelique and I heard a knock on our door. The golden light of a lowering sun tumbled through the cabin windows. Angelique was hemming a new petticoat for her trousseau. I was reading aloud to her from Papa's copy of *Robinson Crusoe*. It's one of my favorite books because it is about an island. I looked up and there was Gavin standing at the open door. I dropped my book and sprang from my chair.

It was not the Gavin who had dressed in the corduroy breeches and cotton shirt of a farmer. It was not White Hawk in Indian dress and war paint. It was someone in between. He wore deerskin trousers, a calico shirt, moccasins, and a buckskin hat such as Mr. Sinclair wore to keep the sun off when he was farming. Around the hat was a beaded band. With his brown skin and long black hair, Gavin was so handsome it quite took my breath away.

"I don't know if I am welcome here," he said, a shy smile on his face. "Your brother and I very nearly killed one another. I must confess when I saw him there before me, I knew at once that I could never fight again in that way."

"It was the same for Jacques," I assured him. "When he realized he was meant to fight you, he decided he would never be a soldier."

We urged Gavin to join us. Angelique gave him a glass of cold buttermilk and a slice of corn-bread. He was cheerful enough but I saw that he had something he wished to tell us.

At last in a grave voice he said, "I have been to talk with Mama and Papa Sinclair. I have not treated them well. I ran away and turned my back on them when they had been so good to me, raising me as their own son." He sighed deeply. "The Sinclairs understand and forgive me. They know I left because I had to discover who I was. I could only learn that from my tribe.

"Now I have news for you." The sober voice became merry. "Can you guess?"

Angelique and I pleaded with him not to tease us but to tell us what he knew.

With a wide grin he said, "Some Indians arrived at L'Arbre Croche last week with word of Jacques."

We were sure from the smile on Gavin's face that the news could not be bad. We urged him to tell us all he knew, for it had been nine long months since Jacques had left us.

Gavin wiped the circle of buttermilk from around his mouth. "The Gauthiers' canoe was seen on Green Bay making its way back here." It was on the Gauthiers' canoe that Jacques had left the island. "It is said that they have been lucky. Because of the war there were few traders. Wherever they went the Indians were pleased to see them and their canoe is loaded with pelts."

When Gavin had done with answering the hundreds of questions we put to him, he said, "Jacques has a surprise for you, but I must leave it for him to reveal." No amount of coaxing would make him relent.

I did not want to part from Gavin so quickly. When he left I accompanied him through the woods to the Sinclairs'. Along the path we found a patch of wild strawberries. The tiny berries, only half the size of my little fingernail, hung like clusters of rubies from their stems. It took much crawling around on our knees to find the berries that were tucked in among the grasses and weeds. We laughed as we fought to snatch away the best berries from one another. I was relieved to see that Gavin had not grown too dignified for such things.

After we had our fill of berries we started once more on the path. I had been thinking over what Gavin had said in our cabin and now I asked, "What did you mean, when you said you could never fight again in that way?"

"The Sinclairs wish me to continue with my education. That is what I mean to do. It is in that way that I will fight."

I was puzzled. "But whom will you fight against? The war is over."

"I will not fight *against* anyone. I will fight *for* my tribe. I have learned from some Potawatami Indians who have fled north that the government has entrapped their chiefs into selling much of their lands for almost nothing. The day will come when the white man will want the land around L'Arbre Croche. Some of our chiefs are weak. They are tempted to give away land for gifts. The government men know how to tempt and they are the men I will fight. But to fight them I must have as much learning as they have.

"Pere Mercier means to send me to his friend Father Gabriel Richard in Detroit. Father Richard has plans to start a university. He has already opened a school for boys and one for girls in Detroit. He wishes that we should have a great school like the one in his native France, where all are welcome to attend."

I was sorry to think that no sooner had Gavin returned to the island than he would be leaving it again. "At least you will not be far," I said.

"I have no wish to be far from the island and the Sinclairs—or from you, Mary."

Gavin's words made me look down to avoid his eyes. It was at that moment that I saw that in our skirmishing about for the berries, the beads that Gavin had given to me had crept out from under my dress where I kept them hidden. There they were for Gavin to see. I was more flurried than ever, but Gavin only laughed and told me he would race me to the Sinclairs'. I wore out my confusion in the running, so that by the time we reached the Sinclairs' farm, I was able to look at Gavin without blushing.

It was the next morning that Belle had her calf. I was on the way to the shed to lead her out to pasture when I heard her making strange sounds. I hurried into the shed to find Belle standing there grunting. The front hooves of the calf had already appeared! In the past Papa or Jacques had been there when the calf was born. Now I was alone. Angelique had gone to St. Anne's that morning, for it was the feast day of St. John the Baptist. It was too late for me to run for the Sinclairs or the MacNeils. I tried to tell myself that everything would be all right. Belle and I would manage.

I patted her and wheedled and coaxed her. After a great deal of straining a nose appeared between the calf's toes. Little by little more of the calf emerged. All of its front legs were out and then there was the whole calf, all slippery and wet and looking half drowned.

The calf just lay there. It didn't seem to be breathing. For a terrible minute I thought it was dead. I remembered a story Papa had told us of what he had done when a newborn calf did not breathe. I shoved Belle aside and kneeling by the calf I pushed on its chest. I let go. I pushed again. Belle was bellowing loudly. I kept pushing and letting up and praying when I had a chance.

It seemed like a miracle when at last I felt the calf's rib cage push up against my hands all by itself. The calf was breathing on its own. With a lot of wobbling it stood up. Belle began to lick the calf clean. She licked so hard with her rough tongue that the calf fell right over and had to wobble up again. Before an hour passed the calf was nursing.

I thought of the thousands and thousands of dead animals the traders would buy. I'd rather be a farmer than a trader anytime. It's true that sometimes you have to kill chickens and pigs and even cows, but most of the time you get in on the start of life.

My happiness didn't last. In two weeks time I had to take the calf to M. André. It was his last payment. I would have given anything to have kept the calf, which now seemed as much mine as Belle's. I asked M. André if I could name it.

"Go ahead if it pleases you," he said. "I never bother to put a name to them for many of them end up on our dinner table."

I shuddered at the terrible image of my dear calf upon a plate. "I'll call it Georgina." That was the name of a heroine in a story I had just read.

"You had better call it George," said M. André, laughing. "This calf is going to be a bull."

18

URING THE LONG, hot summer days I worked from the first crow of the rooster to the whipoorwill's cry at dusk. When they returned I wanted Jacques and Papa to be proud of our farm. Angelique helped as well. She was thinking of her wedding day, though, for she took a great deal of time to wrap herself up in a bonnet and gloves to keep the sun from spoiling her complexion. I was nearly finished before she was ready to start. She did not complain, but I was sure she could not help thinking that in London there would be no fields of corn to hoe.

Because of our work we could not always be on the shore watching for ships and canoes. So it happened that Jacques appeared suddenly when we least expected him. We were picking bugs off the potato plants. All at once he had his arms around us, hugging Angelique and swinging me about like he used to when I was little.

We hardly recognized him. His hair had not been cut for months and hung in curls about his face, which had tanned to the color of walnuts. He was no longer a gangling boy but broader about the shoulders and sturdier of build.

"You two make tolerable farmers," he said, looking about with approval at our planted fields. We grabbed his hands and dragged him around the farm to see what we had accomplished. Even Belle seemed pleased to have him back, switching her tail and rolling her eyes. There was much to tell Jacques of all the things that had happened while he was gone. Angelique said nothing about Lieutenant Cunningham. I did not either, for I thought it was hers to tell.

For his part Jacques told one wondrous story after another with no stopping. "I wish you could have seen the size of the black bear that chased me one night while I was making camp. I ended up on the top of a tree. The Fox River lies between high ridges and runs swiftly. There is a stretch of whitewater that turned our canoe around and around and finally tumbled us out into the water. And buffalo! There is no meat so fine to eat! Dog boiled in maple syrup is pretty tasty, too.

"You must come down and see what we have brought back. Our canoe is loaded with every kind of fur. There are the skins of mink, otter, lynx, wolf, martin, fox, and bear. The pelts will bring the Gauthiers and myself a good sum of money."

As he named the animals I could see them alive and running through the woods and then dead, skinned and stuffed into the canoe and my pleasure in his success was damped a little.

"There was one surprise, though," Jacques said. "I expected to see beavers everywhere upon the rivers. It was not so. The beavers are nearly gone."

I thought that if traders kept heaping their canoes with skins soon there would be no animals at all, but I said nothing, for I would not spoil Jacques' first hours at home. Instead we readied ourselves to hurry down to see what the canoe held and to welcome the Gauthiers.

On the way, Angelique carefully said, "A very *aimable* Lieutenant Cunningham at the fort has been a help to us."

"I dare say he had an eye out for the hen-house and the cow shed," Jacques scoffed.

"No, indeed," said Angelique. "He came to warn us that thieves were planning to steal Belle and sell her to the quartermaster at the fort." Together we told him the story of how we had caught the thieves.

"Well, it may be that there are one or two decent British soldiers, but when they have their muskets pointed at you, they are all the same."

Angelique took a deep breath and then let her words out all in a rush. "You must not say that, Jacques, for Lieutenant Cunningham and I are engaged to be married, indeed we are."

Jacques stopped and stared at her. "Married to a British soldier! To the enemy!"

"He is no longer the enemy," Angelique protested. "The war has ended."

"But you are just a child. How can you think of marrying?"

"I am not a child. I am a year older than you are."

Jacques was strangely silent. Then he shook

his head. "I don't know what Papa will say. For me, I do not think I can sit at the same table with a redcoat, but I will not tell you what you must do with your heart."

We spent the rest of the morning admiring the heaps of furs in the canoe. Jacques had brought Angelique ermine skins to trim a coat. For me there was the skin of a lynx to make into a hat.

That afternoon we showed Jacques off to all our friends. When I saw Gavin and Jacques embrace one another, I was sure at last that the war was over. At the Wests', Emma, who had always admired Jacques, was clearly taken with how manly and comely he had become. "You'll stay here on the island now, won't you, Jacques?" she asked.

"Oh, no. I want to see Papa, and then as soon as fall comes and we are loaded with trading goods, I will be off again."

I was sad myself to think of Jacques leaving again and could understand Emma's disappointment. I knew, too, that she would not wish to be wife to a trader who spent nine months of each year in the company of bears and foxes.

Mr. West, who must have been unmindful of his daughter's affection for Jacques, teased my brother. "If you are always traveling about, how will you get a wife for yourself?"

"I will get one who will travel with me," Jacques answered.

"Surely there can be no woman who would wish to make her way across frozen lakes and through blizzards year after year?" sniffed Elizabeth.

Jacques tossed back his hair and grinned. "There is, and I have found her."

Startled, I asked, "Who is she?"

"She is the daughter of the Sauk chief, Black Wolf. She can paddle a canoe and patch one up as well. She knows how to make snowshoes and skin animals. Besides that she is very pretty and good."

The table was silent. I tried not to look at Emma. Jacques had never guessed how much Emma liked him, so he would not know how he had hurt her. At last Mrs. West asked in a shocked voice, "Do you mean to marry this girl?"

I believe Jacques was quite enjoying how much he had startled everyone. "I certainly hope to marry her," he said, "but her father is against it. Chief Black Wolf said that he would not give his permission for a year. I must come back next year and ask again for her hand. Then he will know that I am serious and will let us get married."

After that we passed a very quiet afternoon and soon made our excuses to the Wests, refusing their kind offer of dinner, explaining that Belle must be milked.

When Jacques and I were alone together in Belle's shed I asked him, "Do you want to marry the Indian girl because she can make snowshoes for you, or do you love her?"

"If you must know, I love her. We were four months at Chief Black Wolf's camp. I saw her there every day. She knows nothing of fashionable dresses or fancy balls, but she knows in what hollow tree a bear is hibernating, or how to call an owl so that it calls back to you, or where to hide so that you can see a pair of otters playing at sliding down a bank. She does not have the fashionable manners that Emma and Elizabeth have, but she has a quiet elegance that is just what you would wish."

Jacques' low voice was filled with affection and told me all I wished to know about his feelings toward Little Cloud. There was one other thing that needed to be said. "Chief Black Wolf and the Sauk fought against the Americans," I reminded him.

"The war is over now," Jacques said.

"That is what Angelique told you and you did not listen. If you can forgive the Sauk then you should be able to forgive the British."

Jacques understood what I was saying. Later that evening I heard him tell Angelique, "I don't mind meeting this Lieutenant Cunningham of yours. If he is going to be a member of our family, he had better get to know me. Then he will have seen the worst of us."

19

*P*APA CAME HOME on July 18, three years and one day after the British army had landed on Michilimackinac. The whole island turned out to see Colonel Anthony Butler and the troops of the Second U.S. Regiment of Riflemen land. A loud cheer went up as they stepped ashore and began their march to the fort, where the British army was waiting to turn the fort over to them. The hundreds of Indians whose canoes accompanied the schooner landed upon the shore and added their cries and musket shots to the celebration. Everywhere American flags that had been laid away were flying again.

Papa and the other islanders who had returned with him were in the last boat to arrive from the schooner. When he came ashore Papa hugged each of us close and then held us away the better to see us. He professed hardly to know us, saying Angelique and I had become quite the young women and Jacques a grown man.

I knew that although there was much joy for Papa in our reunion, concealed beneath the joy was a sorrow. I thought of the battle I had seen and how it had saddened me. I knew Papa had seen many such battles.

Jacques asked why Papa was not in uniform but only wore his corduroy trousers and calico shirt. Papa said, "I was never a regular soldier. I was only a member of the militia at a time when things were desperate. Any hand, however untrained, was welcome. Now I can once again be what I wish to be, a simple farmer. Come and show me what is left of the farm."

As we hurried up the path Papa said, "When I left the island I thought I would be gone only a few months. I could not imagine the war would drag on as it did. Had I guessed how long my time away would be, I would not have left you." His shoulders heaved with a sigh. "There cannot be much remaining of the farm. The work would have been too hard for you."

I could not help teasing Papa. "Yes," I said. "Belle was stolen by the British and the chickens are all eaten and the fields have not been planted." When I saw the sorry look on his face I relented at once. Hastily I said, "It is just as you left it." But I think Papa believed my first story rather than my repair, for as we reached the farm, and he saw the fields planted in corn and the beans climbing up their poles and the turnips and cabbages all leafed out, there was a look of great surprise and pleasure on his face. We showed him the busy henhouse and watched his relief as Belle came moseying across the pasture toward him.

He tried to hide them but we could not help seeing the tears he blinked away. "On a thousand occasions, children, the thought of you and of the farm kept me from despair. It cheered me in victory and sustained me in defeat. I cannot put into words how proud of you I am."

When Papa was done with looking over the farm and we had properly fed him, we begged for stories of the places he had seen and the battles he had been in. Then it was our turn to tell our stories. Imagine Papa's surprise to learn that Jacques had become a trader and had traveled into the wild country of the west.

Papa said, "I do not think you should have left your sisters, Jacques, but in my own long absence from you I set a poor example. I would rather see you choose the settled life of a farmer. Yet in your longing to see more of the world there is something of my own yearning when I left Ireland for the new land of America."

Jacques' only mention of Chief Black Wolf's daughter was that she had been a great help to himself and the Gauthiers. Papa looked closely at him when he said this, for when Jacques mentioned Little Cloud's name, he blushed as red as the scarlet tanager that watched us from the top of a nearby pine.

The story of Lieutenant Cunningham was soon told, for the lieutenant came to say farewell to Angelique. Having turned the fort over to the American forces the British were on their way to nearby Drummond Island. Lieutenant Cunningham would not be there long for he was leaving the army to return to London and his father's business.

Papa saw at once that Angelique and Lieutenant Cunningham were in love. Lieutenant Cunningham apologized to Papa. "I regret, sir, that I could not ask you for your daughter's hand in marriage as I ought to have. I hope you will forgive me and allow me to do so now, for Angelique and I have learned to care for one another."

Papa said that he would say nothing against such a marriage, but he wished to know Lieutenant Cunningham better before he gave his blessing. "I have only just set foot back on the island when I hear my son is about to leave for the west country. Now I learn you are to carry my daughter off to London. You will understand that all of this is too much for me to grasp in so short a time." What Papa was too polite to say was that it was hard on him to have an Englishman for a son-in-law. After all, it was the British who had caused so much trouble in his old country of Ireland.

The next weeks flew by. Papa, with Jacques' help, was busy everywhere on the farm repairing fences in the pasture, building a new pen for the hogs, which the Sinclairs had returned, patching the roof of the henhouse, laying by wood for the winter, and taking Belle to

see Jupiter, for it was time for Belle to have a new calf.

Papa was surprised when I returned the gold five-dollar piece to him. "Is it possible that you managed without spending it?" he said. "Since you have been so thrifty, you shall buy what you wish with it."

"Anything I want?"

"Yes. What will it be? A fine new dress or a four-poster bed for the loft?"

"We have given M. André four calves fo Belle. Could we please buy the last one bac with the five dollars?" I told him how I h delivered George myself. "Besides, it will gr up to be a bull. We won't have to take Belle M. André's anymore. All the rest of the ca will be ours and they will have calves."

Papa laughed but I saw how pleased he "Very well, but it is not what I expected y ask for. I can see I will have to be watchfu no time you will own my farm." I believe relieved. Although Jacques and Angelique be leaving, I would stay on. Together we make the farm prosper.

Lieutenant Cunningham came visit. With the war over the duties of t

on Drummond Island were light. At first Papa was nothing more than coldly polite to the lieutenant, for he did not like the idea of him taking Angelique so far away. But after several visits, Papa had to admit that Lieutenant Cunningham was such a man as would be a good husband to Angelique. Papa could not fail to see all the little fond attentions they showed to one another. I believe he knew as well that Angelique would be happier away from the hard life of the island. Hadn't he told me himself that Angelique was a romantic and that life on a farm might prove too harsh for her? When Lieutenant Cunningham learned that in two weeks' time he was to sail to Montreal and on to England, Papa agreed to the wedding so that Angelique might sail with the lieutenant.

What a flurry there was then! We had to make Angelique's wedding dress and a traveling dress for her. I was to get a new dress as well. It was to be the latest fashion with tight sleeves and little puffs at the shoulders and a high waist. Mrs. Sinclair came to help and so did Mrs. West with Elizabeth and Emma. Elizabeth said she wished she were going to London. Emma only looked at Jacques and said nothing.

The wedding took place at the end of

August. Papa and Jacques and Angelique and I walked to St. Anne's with the sun shining and the wild asters and goldenrod along our path. From the top of a pine tree a white-throated sparrow sang us on our way. Angelique wore a wreath of wild roses in her hair. I had one woven with daisies. Lieutenant Cunningham looked noble in his white breeches, red jacket, scarlet sash, and tall hat with its plume. The sword that he carried was one worn by his father when he was a soldier in India.

Pere Mercier said it was not just a wedding but a joining in peace of America and England. He was very solemn as he said it, but it was hard not to smile at his red face and peeling skin. The perch fishing had been excellent so we knew where the sunburn came from. Afterward at the wedding party Pere Mercier was not so dignified. Tucking up the skirt of his cassock he showed us all a dance that was done at French weddings.

All the officers from the fort attended. They looked splendid in their dress uniforms. M. André played his fiddle and for once Elizabeth had all the dance partners she wished. Emma managed to get Jacques to dance with her. Gavin, who was the handsomest one there in his deerskin jacket trimmed in quillwork and beaded fringes, danced with me twice.

"Your new dress," he said, "becomes you, but I fear you will have grown too stylish to chase about in the woods with me."

"Indeed not," I told him. "I cannot wait to change my clothes! The waist on my dress is so tight I can hardly breathe and my new pumps pinch beyond anything."

"If I write to you, Mary, will you answer my letters?"

I wanted to say at once that nothing would give me greater pleasure, but I was too shy to give away my feelings. "You will have so many new things to see in Detroit that you will not want to spend time on letters to me."

I believe Gavin understood what lay behind my light words, for he put his hand on mine and answered, "I think the things I find in Detroit will not be half so nice as what I have left behind on our island."

Nothing that evening pleased me so much as Gavin speaking of "our" island. It meant that he, too, cared for Michilimackinac and thought of it as his own. If that were so, I could hope that he would one day return to live here. For myself, I could think of living nowhere else.

It was only when Angelique had changed into her traveling clothes and was ready to leave with Lieutenant Cunningham for the schooner, that I had to admit to myself she was really going away. I could not help crying. Angelique promised that she would be back one day to see us. She even coaxed Papa into agreeing to let me visit her in London.

That night, for the first time in my life, I would sleep all alone in the loft. When I opened my chest to take out my nightdress I found a small package carefully done up in paper and ribbon and addressed to me. When I opened it, I found Angelique had left me Mama's book of recipes.

The next evening Gavin came by to say his farewells. By the end of the week he was gone. My only comfort was in looking forward to his letters.

Now it was Jacques' turn to leave. He was helping the Gauthiers gather all of the goods they would give to the Indians in exchange for the Indians' fur pelts. "Now that the war is over," Jacques said, "there are traders everywhere on the island. Soon all the trading goods will be gone. We have already had trouble finding enough blankets to take with us. If the rumor that John Jacob Astor is bringing his American Fur Company to Michilimackinac is true, that is the man I would work for. He will have the largest fur company in the world."

Our farewells to Jacques were not as sad as those to Angelique, for we knew we would see him again in the spring. Perhaps Little Cloud would be with him.

After seeing Jacques off, Papa and I climbed to the west bluff of the island, where we would have a better view. Loaded with trading goods, the Gauthiers' canoe lay low upon the water. From the bluff where we stood it looked like a plaything set upon the great lake.

The sea gulls swooped and arced their way across the sky below us. Autumn was coming on. That morning in the loft I heard acorns falling on the roof. In the pasture Belle's breath came out in little clouds of steam. The leaves of the maple trees were the scarlet we had once seen in the jackets of the British soldiers. Soon the gulls would leave us and winter would come on. This winter with Papa here there would be nothing to fear. In the spring the gulls would return over the water, and so would Jacques and Gavin and someday, Angelique. For on an island the world comes to you over the water.

AUTHOR'S NOTE

This book owes much to the Mackinac State Historic Parks' many excellent publications on the War of 1812. While I have tried to be accurate in fact, this is a story of my imagining after many trips to an island I have grown to love.

Although a hundred and eighty years have passed since the War of 1812 ended, Mackinac Island has changed little. From its hilltop Fort Mackinac still guards the island. Travel, as it was in Mary's day, is by horse and wagon. Gulls and eagles soar over the island still, but the Indian camp is gone and it has been many years since a wolf was seen.